DON'T WORRY, WARRIOR!

10 STRATEGIES TO BATTLE ANXIETY
USING PRACTICAL TOOLS FROM GOD'S WORD

LEVI LUSKO

ILLUSTRATED BY MUTI

Tommy NELSON

An Imprint of Thomas Nelson

Don't Worry, Warrior!

Copyright © 2025 by Levi Lusko

Tommy Nelson, PO Box 141000, Nashville, TN 37214

All rights reserved. No portion of this book may be reproduced, stored in a retrieval system, or transmitted in any form or by any means—electronic, mechanical, photocopy, recording, scanning, or other—except for brief quotations in critical reviews or articles, without the prior written permission of the publisher.

Published by Tommy Nelson, an imprint of Thomas Nelson, 501 Nelson Place, Nashville, TN 37214, USA.

Published in association with the literary agency of Wolgemuth & Wilson.

Tommy Nelson titles may be purchased in bulk for educational, business, fundraising, or sales promotional use. For information, please email SpecialMarkets@ThomasNelson.com.

Scripture quotations marked ERV are taken from the Holy Bible, Easy-to-Read Version. Copyright © 2014 by Bible League International. Used by permission. Scripture quotations marked ICB are taken from the International Children's Bible®. Copyright © 1986, 1988, 1999, 2015 by Thomas Nelson. Used by permission. All rights reserved. Scripture quotations marked NIV® are taken from the Holy Bible, New International Version®, NIV®. Copyright © 1973, 1978, 1984, 2011 by Biblica, Inc.® Used by permission of Zondervan. All rights reserved worldwide. www.zondervan.com. The "NIV" and "New International Version" are trademarks registered in the United States Patent and Trademark Office by Biblica, Inc.®

ISBN 978-1-4002-5324-1 (audiobook)
ISBN 978-1-4002-5320-3 (ePub)
ISBN 978-1-4002-5326-5 (HC)

Library of Congress Control Number: 2025014439

Without limiting the exclusive rights of any author, contributor or the publisher of this publication, any unauthorized use of this publication to train generative artificial intelligence (AI) technologies is expressly prohibited. HarperCollins also exercise their rights under Article 4(3) of the Digital Single Market Directive 2019/790 and expressly reserve this publication from the text and data mining exception.

HarperCollins Publishers, Macken House, 39/40 Mayor Street Upper, Dublin 1, D01 C9W8, Ireland (https://www.harpercollins.com)

Illustrated by MUTI.

Printed in India

25 26 27 28 29 MAI 5 4 3 2 1

Mfr: MAI / Manipal, India / October 2025 / PO #12319668

To Clover Dawn: Watching you bravely fight through worry and rise up as a warrior again and again has been awe-inspiring. I love you!

CONTENTS

Introduction — vii

Strategy 1. Take Charge of Your Mood — 1
Strategy 2. Find the Good in Change — 17
Strategy 3. Learn to Love the You God Made — 35
Strategy 4. Use Your Words for Good — 51
Strategy 5. Learn to Name Your Feelings — 69
Strategy 6. Create Good Habits — 85
Strategy 7. Choose to Be Brave — 105
Strategy 8. Plan for Life's Responsibilities — 123
Strategy 9. Give Your Worries to God — 141
Strategy 10. Trust God in Hard Times — 161

Afterword: God Has Your Back — 179
Notes — 181

INTRODUCTION

A famous cowboy once said that being brave isn't about never feeling afraid but about saddling up your horse to ride again after you've fallen off.[1] The goal isn't *never* feeling scared; it's being brave *when* you feel afraid. Through so much of my life, worry, anxiety, and even panic have been parts of my story. For a long time this weighed on me—I felt bad about feeling bad. Through biblical study, God has helped me see that I don't need to be embarrassed about this struggle. So many biblical heroes such as Elijah, Moses, Jeremiah, Esther, and many others struggled with scary thoughts, bad moods, and even dark nights of doubt. Hundreds of verses speak about fear, anxiety, depression, and bad dreams, and none of them say you should be ashamed of struggling with these things or that, if you love God, you won't ever have bad days. If anything, the presence of these difficult emotions is proof that you are human and that you need God's help. In Psalm 73:26, David said, "My flesh and my heart may fail, but God is the strength of my heart and my portion forever" (NIV). This verse has encouraged me in many hard moments.

This is not a book that is going to make difficult emotions and moments in your life go away. What I want to tell you in these pages isn't a magic pill or a secret to a stress-free life. Even if there were such a thing (there isn't), you wouldn't really want that—not deep down—because in our hardships is when God comes close and helps us grow into who we were born to be. "The LORD is a warrior; the LORD is his name" (Exodus 15:3 NIV), and you were created in His image. That means you are called to be a warrior too! How are you ever going to get there if you don't go through hard things? (Hint: You can't. Battles are sort of warrior territory.)

This book is all about what to do when you feel anxious. The Bible tells us to not worry. Philippians 4:6 says, "Do not be anxious about anything, but in every situation, by prayer and petition, with thanksgiving, present your requests to God" (NIV). When you have scary emotions, choose to put your trust in God and saddle up your horse anyway—even after you have fallen off. You will then grow into the warrior God created you to be.

There are ten strategies in this book that demonstrate hard-fought lessons I have learned along my own warrior path. They have helped me and my family big-time, and I am excited to share them with you! Along the way I will introduce you to two characters, Luca and Coral, who will face struggles of their own. Their stories show examples of the lessons we are learning lived out by people your age.

Thank you for reading this book, and I pray you know how loved you are by the Good Shepherd, who is with you on your good days as well as your bad ones!

Levi Lusko, a.k.a. your fellow warrior

STRATEGY 1

TAKE CHARGE OF YOUR MOOD

"Dad, help! Where are my lucky socks?! I can't find my lucky socks!"

It was Saturday morning, and Luca had torn his room apart. He'd already put on his favorite shin guards, soccer shorts, and jersey—a blue-and-white Lionel Messi jersey, of course—but his favorite socks were nowhere to be found. He'd looked in his dresser, his closet, and even the dryer. His nose wrinkled in confusion. *Where have they gone?*

"I'll look in my drawer to see if your socks got mixed with mine," Dad called to Luca from down the hall. Luca got down on his hands and knees and searched under the bed. No socks down there—just dust bunnies, a few LEGO bricks, and an action figure he'd forgotten about.

Today was a big day for Luca: the day of the soccer tryouts he'd been practicing for all summer. He was already worried about how the day would go, and the thought of facing tryouts without his lucky socks made him even more nervous.

His dad popped his head into Luca's bedroom. "Can't find 'em, Chipper," Dad said, using Luca's special nickname. "Might be time to pick some other socks that are just as lucky."

Luca, frustrated, saw the digital clock on his nightstand and knew his dad was right. He needed to be at the field soon, and he still needed to eat breakfast. He stood up, walked to the dresser, and found another pair that would have to work. He gave them a sniff. Fortunately, they didn't stink too bad.

Dad and Luca went downstairs and found Mom and Luca's little sister, Anna, at the kitchen table. Mom had made some pancakes and set out a glass of orange juice for Luca.

"We've got a few minutes, Luca. Want some breakfast?"

"I do. Thanks, Mom." Luca pulled out a chair and sat. The fresh pancakes made the whole room smell like a bakery. He doused them in syrup, took a big bite, then picked up his juice glass to wash it all down. But when he reached over his plate to set down the glass, he knocked over the bottle of maple syrup.

Slosh!

The sugary liquid oozed down Luca's clean jersey and onto his shorts. "Oh, no!" he shrieked, jumping up from his chair. Dad also jumped up and grabbed a dish towel, but it was too late. Luca's favorite jersey was now sticky and gross.

"Run and change, honey. We need to leave in five," his mom said.

As Luca hurried back upstairs to change into his *not*-favorite jersey, his feelings began to swirl. Without his lucky socks *or* his favorite jersey, how would he possibly do his best today? His mood was already beginning to plummet, and the day had barely begun. He ran to the closet and found another old jersey that would have to work, then yanked off the dirty shirt and shorts. "Sorry, Messi," he mumbled, tossing the sticky jersey into the clothes hamper. Then he pulled on fresh clothes and sprinted back down the stairs.

His parents and Anna were already cleaning up the kitchen table.

"Can I finish eating?" Luca asked. He wasn't sure if it was hunger or nervousness making his stomach feel weird. Maybe it was both.

"Yes, but hurry," his dad said. "We don't want you to be late."

Without sitting down, Luca scarfed down as many bites of pancake as he could. In a matter of a minute, he cleaned his whole plate. Maybe that was a bad idea, though, because right away, he felt a little queasy.

As he climbed into the van with his family, Luca couldn't help but feel a little bad for himself. Nothing had gone right today, and tryouts hadn't even started. As they headed down the road toward the field, he worried the rest of the day would be just as unlucky as his morning. His hands felt a bit shaky, and he wondered why he was already sweating. Luca felt his brow furrowing and a scowl making its way across his face.

BEWARE OF EVIL LEVI

When was the last time you were in a really bad mood? Did your day start out anything like Luca's? On crummy days, nothing seems to go your way—and just when things seem to be bad enough, something else happens to make you feel even *worse*. Maybe you had a fight with your parents about how much screen time you should get. Maybe you tripped on your shoelace and ate the pavement in front of your friends. Maybe your little brother threw your library books in the toilet, or you worked really hard on your science project and didn't get the grade you thought you should. All sorts of things can put us in a funk—so you're not the only person to ever feel this way. Even a warrior in training has a bad day now and then.

How do you know you're in a bad mood? I don't know about you, but when I'm in a funk, I almost become a different person—an evil version of myself I like to call "Evil Levi." It's almost like the normal version of me gets taken hostage by the evil version. When Evil Levi is in charge, he's angry and annoyed, he's snippy and mean to others, and he can't see anything but the bad parts of his day. He feels sorry for himself and spreads his bad mood to everyone who happens to be near him. Eventually, after letting his bad mood completely take over, Evil Levi decides to give up on the rest of the day. *This day is spoiled*, he thinks. *I'll just have to try again tomorrow.*

You've felt that way, haven't you? As though so much of the day has been wasted that there's no use trying to make good decisions. *Tomorrow is a new day. This one's no good.*

Most of the time, we find ourselves in a bad mood when something bad happens to us. When we stub our toes or get picked on at school, those things can make us feel powerless and sad. But what if I were to tell you that you *aren't* powerless—that you have way more say in how you think and feel than you probably ever knew?

You are brave. You are strong. And I want to train you to take control of your life in all the ways you can—and that often starts with choosing your mood. You're becoming a warrior, and before you can be strong on the outside, you must be strong on the inside.

THE THINGS YOU'RE IN CHARGE OF

The adults in your life make a lot of choices for you, like where you live, where you go to school, and sometimes even what you eat or wear.

(Raise your hand if you've ever fought with your mom about your outfit for school picture day!) It's your parents' or guardians' job to make good decisions that will keep you safe and healthy while you're growing up. But as you grow up, young warrior, you will get to make more and more decisions for yourself. In other words, *you* get to be in charge.

Still, you may be tempted to think that your mood—the way you feel—isn't one of the things you get to be in charge of. Something gross, sad, or annoying happens—something you didn't choose—and it puts you in a bad mood, right? But even though we may not be in control of the things that happen to us, we *are* in control of how we think about them and respond to them. Your brain belongs to you, after all. And part of growing up is learning to take charge of your own thoughts and moods.

Let me give you an example. When I was in school, I took an art class. It was a lot of fun—paints, pencils, canvases, and creative messes everywhere. I looked forward to this class every day. We each had a little cubby where we would paint, draw, sketch, or color for forty-five minutes. My teacher was a kind woman named Mrs. Losey, and on occasion she allowed us to bring in music to listen to while we worked.

Here's the funny part, though. I have a lot of memories of going to class in a bad mood. But no matter what had happened earlier in the day to fray my nerves or tank my spirit, I never left my art class in a funk.

Why do you think that is?

Now that I'm older, I understand why art class made me feel so much better. It was a safe place where I could take deep breaths, do something fun and creative, and reset my thoughts and mood. I could put aside all the terrible, horrible, no-good things from earlier in the day and focus instead on something I enjoyed. No wonder I loved going to art class so much!

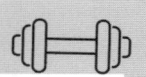

Part of growing up is discovering the activities, habits, and places that make us feel better. Maybe for you, riding your bike or spending time with your grandad makes you feel peaceful and calm. Or maybe you like reading books, playing with your dog, or listening to music. The things you love and enjoy are as unique to you as your fingerprints because God made you unlike anyone else He's ever made.

As I said, your list is unique because *you* are unique. God made you that way! Now let's talk about how to use what we know about ourselves to make better decisions about our moods.

> ## TACTICAL TRAINING
>
> Let's take a quick break here to brainstorm a list of what tends to make you happy and ideas to improve your mood.
>
> I am happiest when I'm
>
> _____
> [INSERT A POSITIVE ACTIVITY.]
>
> When I'm in a bad mood, being in
>
> _____
> [INSERT A PLACE YOU LOVE.]
> usually makes me feel better.
>
> When I'm anxious or worried,
>
> _____
> [INSERT A POSITIVE ACTIVITY.]
> can calm me down.

CHANGE YOUR MOOD, CHANGE THE GAME

I'm a grown-up, and it's still hard for me to control my mood sometimes—even though I've had a lot of practice! But warriors have to control their emotions. Why? You may not think your mood matters to anyone but you, but have you ever been around someone who just seems to be mad, annoyed, or snippy *all the time*? Their bad moods affect *them* the most, of course, but their sourness can also spread to you. So it's important to realize that learning how to better control your mood will not only make *you* feel better, but it will also make everyone else's day a little better too. Talk about a game changer!

I've got three ideas for you, and I hope you'll try them all. Especially if you tend to worry a lot or get upset often, I hope some of these strategies will help you battle the bad feelings that can ruin your day.

Step 1: Switch Positions

Have you ever participated in a sport and thought you were terrible at it—until you switched positions? All you needed was a new place to play! Moods can be similar. Sometimes "switching positions" by going to a new place or changing your circumstances can take you one step closer to a better mood.

At your age, you're still not in charge of many of your circumstances (such as where you go to school or where you live). But when you find yourself in a situation that's making you anxious or upset, think about what you *can* change. Here are some examples:

If you're in your older brother's room and he's being mean to you—do you *have* to stay in his room? Or can you find somewhere else to go?

If you're outside at recess and your friend says something mean to you—do you *have* to stand there and take it? Or can you walk away and play with someone else?

If someone at your lunch table is a bully to you or someone else—do you *have* to keep sitting at that table? Or can you ask an adult to help you find a new group of people to sit with?

If you're taking dance classes but you get nervous and panic before each lesson—do you *have* to keep taking lessons? Or can you talk to your parents about trying another activity instead? Or are there calming practices you can do before your dance class starts to help soothe your nerves?

It's true that you can't change all your circumstances, but if you know a situation is ruining your mood on a regular basis, talk to a trusted adult about how you can "switch positions" to avoid those situations in the future.

Step 2: Think Positive

In the Bible, Paul the apostle told us to "think about what is good and worthy of praise. Think about what is true and honorable and right and pure and beautiful and respected" (Philippians 4:8 ERV). These are some fancy words that mean *"think about good things."* Do you imagine that thinking about good things—the things that bring you happiness and peace—could help you when you're feeling down?

I admit, this one is a bit harder to master—in fact, I'm still trying! But it *is* possible to have a better mood when you choose to think positive. Let me give you another example here.

Let's say you did poorly on your math homework, and you feel bad about it. (Relatable!) You have two choices now.

Option 1: Spend the rest of the week feeling bad about your grade and telling yourself, "I am so bad at math—there's no way I'll ever be good at it."

Option 2: Spend the rest of the week trying to figure out what you didn't understand about your assignment. Ask your teacher or your parents for help and tell yourself, "If I try harder this week, I'll do better next time."

Which is the better option? Which is more likely to lead to better grades *next* week and a better mood *this* week? Which choice are you more likely to make?

Taking charge of our thoughts is not easy. It doesn't always come naturally. But when we choose not to feel sorry for ourselves and not to dwell on negative things, we are choosing a more positive path—one that almost always leads to a better mood.

Step 3: Talk to God

In the Psalms, a book full of poems and songs, King David wrote about how God, his Father, had taken care of him. One day he said to God: "Your help made me so happy. Give me that joy again. Make my spirit strong and ready to obey you" (Psalm 51:12 ERV). God cared for David when he was feeling down and afraid—and He will do the same for you!

Next time you find yourself in a bad mood, why not talk to God about it? Tell Him what you're feeling and ask for His help. God loves nothing more than to hear the voice of His young warrior, and He knows just what you need. Want to practice a prayer you can use anytime you're down in the dumps and need a little encouragement from God?

Dear God, thank You for loving me and caring about my feelings. Today I'm upset about _____, and I need Your comfort and care. Will You help me feel better, and will You change my attitude? Help me to see that the rest of this day can still be good. Amen.

> **WARRIOR CHALLENGE**
>
> Taking deep breaths may sound simple—I mean, it is!—but did you know it's one of the best ways to calm yourself when you're upset? Next time you catch yourself becoming the version of you that you don't want to be (looking at you, Evil Levi), try breathing in for five seconds, breathing out for five seconds, and waiting for five seconds. Repeat as needed. You should feel yourself returning to normal with each deep breath you take.

Whenever you face a bad mood, don't let it control you! Look in the mirror, remind yourself that you are a warrior in training, and work out your inner strength by crushing your bad mood to dust.

By the time Luca was on the soccer field, his nerves had gotten the best of him. Normally a confident and strong player, he lined up with the other kids to practice shots and missed five goals in a row. Before long he was fumbling passes and tripping over his own feet. After having the ball stolen from him for the third time, he threw his hands in the air with frustration.

When the players were all given a ten-minute water break, Luca trudged over toward his family, who were sitting on the bleachers along the field. His shaggy brown hair was dripping with sweat, and his tired legs seemed to weigh a thousand pounds apiece.

"I'm ready to quit," he said, taking a bottle of water from his mom's hand. "My tryout is obviously wrecked. I'm not sure why I ever thought I was good at soccer."

"Hey, that's my son you're talking about!" said his dad. "You've been practicing for this all summer. Maybe you just need to change your attitude. If you go out there thinking you're going to play badly, you probably will."

Luca scoffed. "Hold up. You're blaming my *attitude* for this?"

Mom took Luca by the shoulders and looked him in the eyes. "Listen, kiddo. I know you're frustrated. Things haven't gone your way today. But what Dad's trying to say is *you* get to decide what happens for the rest of this tryout. You can focus on what has gone wrong, or you can choose to start fresh. You have a whole hour left to show everyone what you can do. Why not try to forget about your mistakes and think about what can go right? We believe in you, Luca. Try to believe in yourself too."

As he wiped sweat from his forehead, Luca thought about his parents' words. He knew he had a choice: to give up or try again. He really did love soccer, and he really wanted to make the team—so the idea of quitting suddenly sounded a little worse than the idea of trying his best. He took a deep breath and another long gulp of water. "Okay," he said. "I've got this."

"Way to go, Chipper!" his dad hollered in a way-too-loud voice. "That's my boy!"

Luca couldn't help but laugh. As he trotted back across the field and rejoined the rest of the players, he tried to think positively instead of

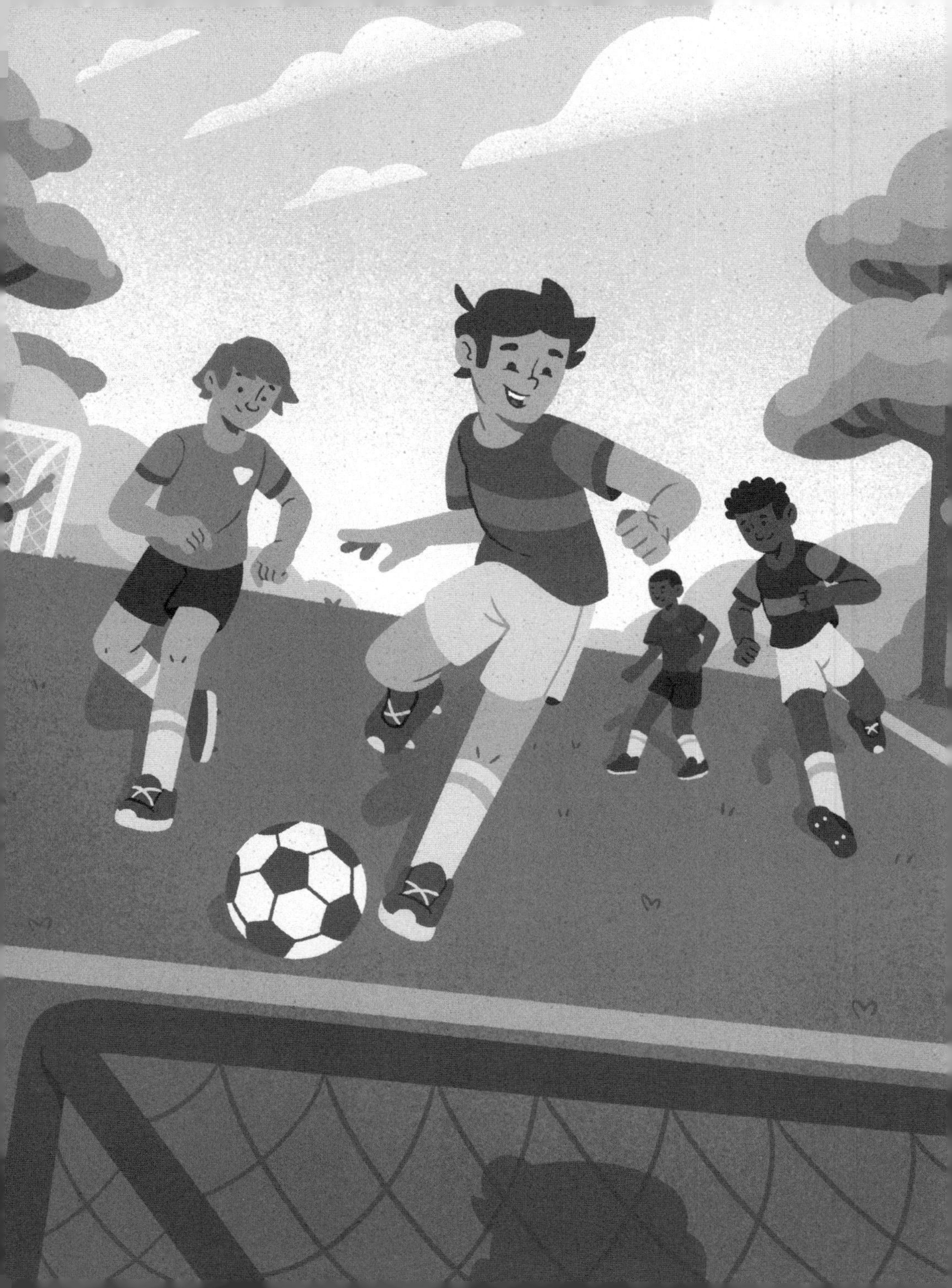

assuming he would fail. Before long, the coaches blew their whistles, and Luca started kicking the ball a little harder and a little straighter. He made a couple of shots he hoped would impress the coaches. He stopped focusing on the mistakes he had made and started running faster. Soon, he found himself having fun again. His mood had gone from bad to better, all because he chose to focus on the good.

After the last whistle was blown, Luca high-fived some of the other players and sprinted back to his family. They all gave him hugs even though he was gross and sweaty, and his little sister, Anna, bounced on her toes and clapped. Though Luca was unsure of the outcome, he was grateful for his supportive family and was sure he had tried his best. As they walked through the park back to the van, Luca's dad gave his shoulder a squeeze.

A few days later, when Luca found out he had officially made the team, his family took him out to celebrate at his favorite pizza place. As they were driving home, stomachs full and spirits high, he looked down at his feet and saw something green poking out from under the seat in front of him. He reached down and pulled his lucky socks out from their hiding spot. "Look what I found!" he called out. "They were here this whole time!"

His mom turned and faced him from the front seat, then laughed at the wadded-up socks in his fist. "Just goes to show you that luck isn't real, kiddo. I'd say you did just fine without them."

His mom winked, and Luca smiled. Knowing he had done his best and succeeded felt a lot better than believing in luck anyway.

GET READY FOR BATTLE

Think about your last terrible, horrible, no-good day—when nothing went according to plan. Reimagine that day with a strategy or two you learned from this chapter. What could you have done differently? How might your day have been better if you had taken control of your mood?

STRATEGY 2

FIND THE GOOD IN CHANGE

Coral had *not* wanted to move away.

Until a few weeks ago, Texas had been Coral's home. Her friends were in Texas. Her *abuelita*, her grandma, was in Texas. Even her favorite park—a little playground around the corner from her house—was in Texas. So when her parents told her over the summer that her dad had accepted a job in another state, she had understandably been pretty devastated.

That same afternoon, she'd gone to her grandmother's house down the block and cried and cried. She rested her head in her abuelita's lap, and her abuelita stroked her long black hair.

"*Mi nieta*, my granddaughter, you are going to be just fine in a new place!" she said. "You are a sweet, smart girl with a big heart. You will make new friends and have new adventures in your new town."

"But I will miss the friends I already have," Coral said. She wiped the tears from her cheeks with the back of her hand. "And what about you, Abuelita? I will miss *you* the most!"

"Oh, hush, hush," her grandmother said. "Your Tía Serena will bring me to see you all the time. The drive is not so far. And you will call me on the phone and show me your face on the screen every day if you want to."

"You mean FaceTime, Abuelita?"

Her grandmother patted her head. "Yes, mi nieta. That's what I mean!" She laughed.

Packing up the house she'd grown up in had made Coral even sadder than before. As Coral and her mother filled a big cardboard box with the art supplies she kept in the room she shared with her sister and brother, her mother tried to cheer her up.

"You know, Coral, your new school will have so many art classes for you," she said. "Drawing, painting . . . The school even has a pottery teacher! You will have more opportunities to be creative than ever before." She carefully packed some of Coral's sketchbooks and pencils in with her stuffed animals.

Coral nodded but didn't say a word. She couldn't bring herself to get excited about anything while she was still so sad about what she'd be leaving behind.

But Mom kept going.

"The house we're moving into is right around the corner from a big park with a playground and fields for sports. And your new bedroom, which will be *all yours*, will be even bigger than this one! The closet has a little more space, and your window looks out over the garden—"

"I get it, Mom!" Coral yelled, throwing a squishy toy into another box. It felt kinda good to throw something, so she threw another one just as hard. "Our new house is gonna be *so great*, and my new school is gonna be *so great*, but what if I just want to stay here? What if I don't *want* new friends or a new place to live? What if I don't want to leave Abuelita and my cousins? What if I *hate* the new place?"

Coral plopped down on her beanbag chair, put her hands over her face, and sighed.

IN THE PITS (OF THE OCEAN)

Maybe you've been in a situation like Coral's, where you had to move from one place to another. Maybe you've started at a new school or experienced some other big changes in your family. Or maybe you've experienced other disappointments—such as not getting the gift you wanted for your birthday, being unable to play on a team, or not getting that part in the play. Big changes and disappointments are not easy to deal with—and they can sometimes lead to you feeling sad, lonely, hopeless, or stuck.

Do you remember the story of Jonah in the Bible? You know, the guy from the Old Testament who took a ride in the belly of a big fish? The fact that he got swallowed by a sea creature is (understandably!) the thing we tend to remember most about him—but the story of Jonah can teach us a lot about dealing with change *and* disappointment. So let's back up in the story for a minute, okay?

The book of Jonah begins with God asking Jonah to go on a trip: "Nineveh is a big city," God said. "I have heard about the many evil things the people are doing there. So go there and tell them to stop doing such evil things" (Jonah 1:2 ERV). We know from the rest of the story that Jonah did *not* want to go to Nineveh, because the next thing he did was hop on a boat to a totally different place. "Jonah tried to run away from the LORD," the Bible tells us (v. 3 ERV). And since God sees and knows everything, He knew that Jonah was trying to avoid what He had asked him to do!

When a big storm came over Jonah's ship, he confessed to the other people on board that he had been trying to run away from God—so they threw him into the ocean! You may already know what happened next:

"When Jonah fell into the sea, the Lord chose a very big fish to swallow Jonah. He was in the stomach of the fish for three days and three nights" (v. 17 ERV).

I think it's fair to say that being in a fish's belly for three days gives you some time to think about your choices! Jonah prayed to God and asked for His help, and because God is forgiving and good, He told the fish to puke out Jonah onto the shore (Jonah 2:10). The idea of being puked out of a fish is pretty weird, but Jonah seemed to have learned his lesson. When God asked Jonah one more time to go back to Nineveh, Jonah did as he was told—and the people of Nineveh listened to him!

What impresses me is that Jonah eventually came around and agreed to go. Sure, it took an extended trip to SeaWorld, but he eventually trusted God and followed where God led him. In the end, the people of Nineveh got to know God in a way they never had before—and their futures were forever changed. When Jonah's no became a yes, God was able to accomplish great things because of his faithfulness.

THE BATTLE AGAINST BIG FEELINGS

As you've probably figured out by now, life doesn't always go your way. You disagree with your parents about bedtime or the people you're allowed to hang out with. Your teacher gives you homework. You get glasses or braces. Your big sister says something rude to you, and when you respond, your parents tell *you* to stop being a brat. ("But *she* started it!" you want to say.)

Or maybe you're dealing with other disappointments or struggles—like your parents getting a divorce or, like Coral, moving to a new city. Hard things can happen at any age, and they will lead to big feelings. Learning to handle these feelings is not easy—but it's a huge part of growing up, and of becoming a warrior.

Actually, you can think of handling disappointments and big feelings as a kind of battle, and it's a battle we all (no matter our age!) have to learn how to fight every day. I wish I could tell you that winning the battle is a piece of cake, but it can be really, *really* hard.

> **WARRIOR CHALLENGE**
>
> Have you ever watched a boxing match? If you don't know much about the sport, it might just seem like a lot of punching and jabbing and no real planning. But the truth is, a *ton* of practice happens before the fight. Spend some time researching "boxing moves" online with a trusted adult. How many combinations can you find? How many different types of punches? Maybe try a few yourself (in the air—*not on your sister*!). Next time you as a young warrior are "in the ring" with big feelings, imagine boxing them away, one strategic punch at a time.

YOU'RE THE BOSS

As we said in the last chapter, sometimes we can't change our circumstances. Despite what we do, things happen that we can't change or control. But part of growing up is learning how to handle our feelings when things don't go our way. For example, let's say you had planned to wear a certain costume to a costume party for weeks, but then the package got lost on the way. Now it's not going to show up, and you have nothing to wear.

Which of the following is an appropriate response to your disappointment?

a. Feel sorry for yourself
b. Beat yourself up for not picking out a costume at the store
c. Cry all day, telling yourself the party isn't worth going to anymore
d. Feel sad for a little while, remind yourself that disappointing things happen sometimes, and then begin making a new costume on the fly

All these responses are natural—but only one makes the best of a bad situation. Only one might lead you to feel better. And only one will put you on the path to positive progress. If you chose *D*, then you are truly a warrior who chose to make the best of the worst!

You may be thinking, *But it's really hard to change how I feel!* That's true—but did you know you are the boss of what you think? Listen to me carefully: Negative thoughts can't lead to a positive life. You probably never wake up and think, *I want to have a bad day* or *I want to be a bummer to be around.* But we all have allowed ourselves to think the kinds of thoughts that lead to a negative day.

That means you can change the way you feel, by changing the way you think. I'm not talking about ignoring your emotions or pretending you don't feel a certain way but rather letting God give you a new perspective. Your feelings are real, but they are not the boss of you.

So how do we become better at battling our negative thoughts? Here are a few ways to practice.

Look for the Good

Have you ever heard of looking for the "silver lining"? The expression refers to clouds during a rainstorm. Sometimes, when the sun is trying to peek from behind a dark cloud, you can see a bright line—a silver lining—surrounding the cloud's edge. While it may be raining cats and dogs on your head, a silver lining is a reminder that the sun is *always* there, ready to shine again—even when it seems like the rain will never stop.

> **THINK LIKE A WARRIOR**
>
> Do you know how rainbows are formed? The simple answer is light is reflected through a raindrop. Here's the thing: It takes both rain *and* light to make a rainbow. If you have a perfectly sunny day without rain—you guessed it: no rainbow. So on your next "rainy day," when nothing seems to be going the way you planned or expected, remember that a rainbow could be just around the corner. All you need to do is find the light.

Looking for the good in something is a *choice*. It's a skill to practice, like learning to blend lines in a sketch or mastering a complicated dance move. The more you do it, young warrior, the easier it gets. Here are some examples:

> Nintendo Switch broken? *Good. I'll spend the afternoon FaceTiming my grandma instead.*
> Big baseball game delayed? *Good. That means I'll have extra time to practice pitching.*
> It's raining again? *Good. I love the smell of rain.*
> They're out of maple-glazed donuts at Dunkin'? *Good. That means I can try something new!*

Try it for yourself. Find the good in each of the following scenarios:

Something that annoys me: _____.
    The silver lining: _____.
Something that disappointed me recently: _____.
    The silver lining: _____.

Next time you feel yourself getting down in the dumps, try to remember to search for that silver lining. Before you know it, you might just find yourself feeling a lot better.

Say What You Feel

Grown-ups don't know everything all the time, but they can be good at seeing the positive in a situation even if you can't.

If something happened at school that has left you disappointed, tell your mom, dad, grandparent, aunt, uncle, or guardian about it. Or talk to a trusted teacher or counselor if you have one. Do your best to describe your situation and use your words to paint a picture of how you feel. Sometimes just naming your feelings is a big first step toward feeling better about what you're going through.

Give It to God

God wants to hear from you anytime you want to talk. And guess what? He, too, can help you see the bright side of a bad situation. Not sure what words to use? That's okay. Just do your best and know that God knows how you feel, even if you're not quite sure how to describe the feelings yourself.

Let's try a few sample prayers together.

Dear God, I'm having a bad day, and my spirits are down in the dumps. Can You help me see the positive side of this situation?

Dear God, will You show me how this bad situation might get better? While I may be disappointed today, what good may come from this?

It's true that you have a God who causes goodness and mercy to follow you all the days of your life (Psalm 23:6). That's pretty cool, right? God is creative—after all, He created *the whole world*—so He can help you come up with some pretty creative, positive-minded perspectives on your challenging situation. And choosing those better perspectives makes you a stronger and wiser warrior. With the right perspective, you'll be in a good mindset to face your next challenge.

In her family's new house, Coral had a bedroom all to herself—no more sharing with her big brother and younger sister—just as her mother had said. The window in her room looked out over the backyard and a garden full of zinnias, butterfly bushes, and cheerful black-eyed Susans that seemed to bop around in the breeze.

Saying goodbye to her old house, her friends, and her family had been one of the hardest things Coral had ever done. As they'd driven out of the only neighborhood she'd ever known, Coral had tried to take in all the familiar sights one last time. Tears had pricked the corners of her eyes as they drove away from the place she had loved. *How will my new home compare to this one?* she had wondered. She had known what she was leaving behind, but she had wondered what, exactly, she was heading toward.

Now, at last, she knew. Along with her family, she was beginning to explore her new house and hometown a little at a time.

Before she unpacked all her clothes and toys, her parents took her to the hardware store. "Pick out a few colors," her dad said. "We think you should paint your room however you want."

Opting for something vibrant, she chose an assortment of blue shades and painted her own version of an ocean and its waves. As she ran her paintbrush along the walls, creating a beautiful swirling effect with her mixture of paints, she couldn't help but smile at her work. Sure, this wasn't her old room, and she still missed her friends and her family back in Texas. But so far, this place wasn't so bad. As she swished her brush back and forth, she chose to think about the good things about her new home.

Classes started at Coral's new school soon after she and her family

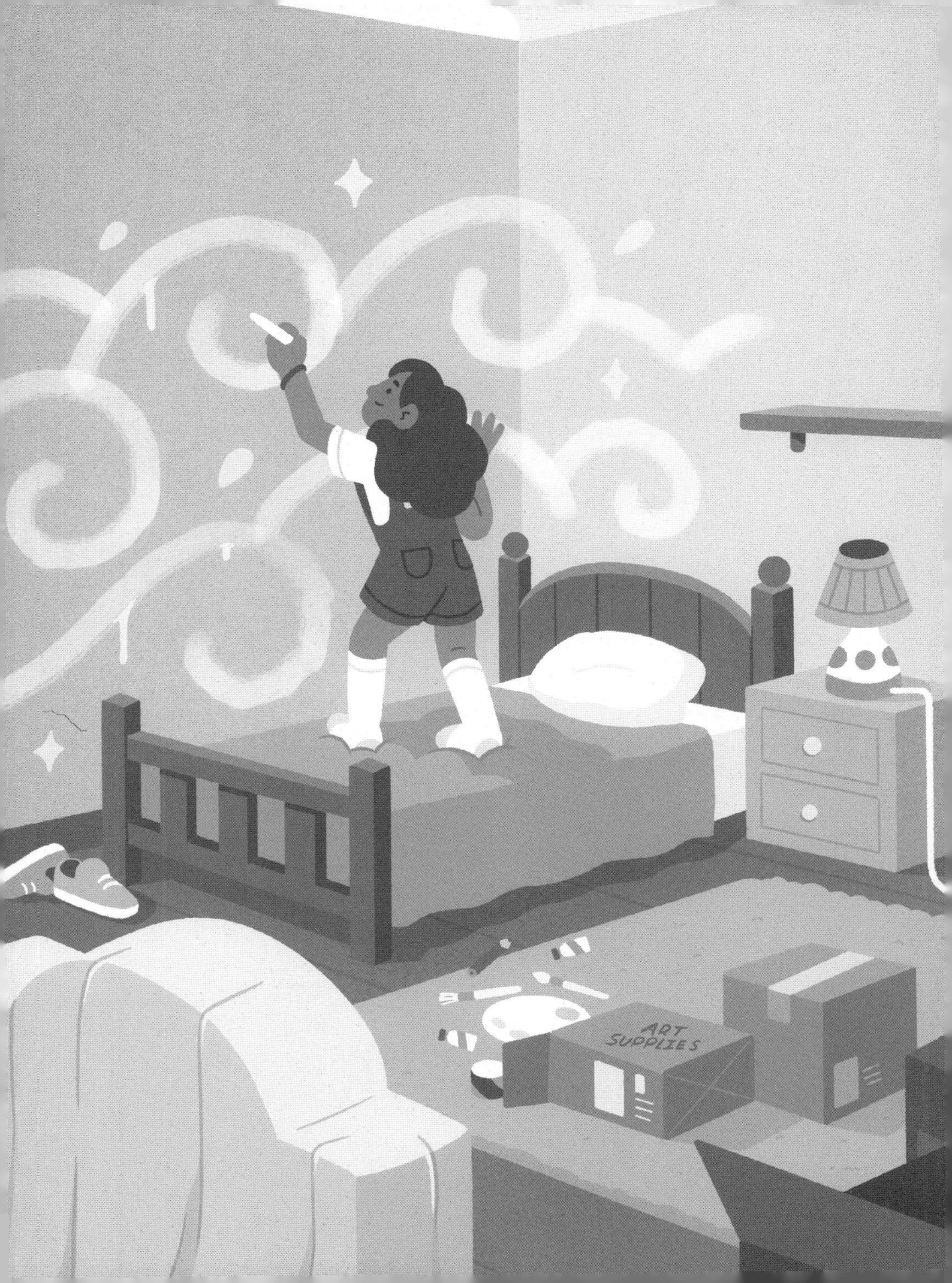
ART SUPPLIES

moved into their new house. She had been nervous about making new friends, but on her first day, a couple of girls from her homeroom asked her to sit with them at lunch. They seemed friendly and nice. They asked Coral a lot of questions about herself, including where she'd moved from. And they complimented the stack of beaded bracelets she wore on her left arm. Coral off took two of the bracelets and handed them to the girls.

"Here. Do you want these?" she asked. "I have tons of beads at home and make more bracelets all the time."

"Really?!" the girls squealed. They smiled from ear to ear, pulled the bracelets on their wrists, and thanked Coral for sharing with them. Since then, Coral had sat with them at lunch every day.

A couple of weeks later, her grandmother and aunt visited. When they pulled into the driveway, Coral ran out and hugged them both as tight as she could. Then she showed them her finished room—all spirals of blue and white waves—and they *oohed* and *aahed* at her work.

The next day, Coral and her abuelita took a walk to the park around the corner from her house. They sat down on a bench shaded by a big, leafy magnolia tree with a nice view of the playground and the soccer fields.

"So, mi nieta," her grandmother asked, "are things any better than you expected here?"

Coral sighed. "I miss you, Abuelita," she said. "And I do miss home. But things are not so bad here. Not really."

Her grandmother put an arm around her. "Changes are hard, mi nieta," she said. "And I know this is not what you wanted. But your parents had good reasons for bringing you here. I hope you are starting to see those reasons for yourself."

As they gazed out at the park from their spot on the bench, Coral noticed a shaggy-haired boy dribbling a soccer ball down the sidewalk. When he neared, she thought she recognized him from her school. She didn't know his name, and his focus was on his footwork and his control of the ball. But when he happened to pause and look her direction, a smile broke out on his face. He tossed up a wave, and Coral waved back. Then the boy kept on moving down the sidewalk, around the bend in the path, and out of Coral's sight.

"Do you want to hear a secret, Coral?" her grandmother asked.

"Of course!" Coral snuggled up next to her grandmother, who smelled of her usual cinnamon and vanilla.

"A long, long time ago, my own abuelita taught me something I never forgot," her grandmother said. "She told me that wherever you look, that's what you see."

Coral blinked and scrunched her brow. "Huh? I don't get it."

Her grandmother playfully pinched Coral's arm. "Patience, mi nieta! I'm not done with the story!"

Coral giggled. "Okay, okay, keep going."

"If you turn your head and choose to focus on that puddle"—she pointed to a big, blotchy, muddy puddle in the grass—"you will not enjoy the view. But if you look over there at that little patch of flowers instead"—she turned her head and gestured across the park toward a little shade garden—"you'll be focused on something prettier. Something lovelier."

Coral thought about her grandmother's words for a moment. "Are you telling me to notice the pretty things, Abuelita?"

"In a way. I'm saying you can *choose* what you see—and if you have a choice between looking at something good or something bad, your heart will be happier if you choose the good things around you."

Coral's grandmother leaned down and kissed her on the top of the head.

"I'm praying for you, mi nieta," her grandmother said, patting her shoulder.

"I pray for you too, Abuelita," Coral said.

Each night since her family had arrived, Coral and her mother had prayed before bedtime, asking God to help them be happy in their new home. Her mother had asked for contentment, and Coral had asked for help making friends. So far, God had helped her find *two* new friends. She hoped He would help her find some more.

No, this place doesn't quite feel like home yet, she thought. *But maybe one day soon it will.*

GET READY FOR BATTLE

What's a change in your life or your family's life that rocked your world the way this move affected Coral's? How did that change make you feel in the moment? How does it make you feel now? Have you found a silver lining yet? If not, spend a little time trying to find it—maybe you can even find two!

STRATEGY 3

LEARN TO LOVE THE YOU GOD MADE

Can I tell you something embarrassing?

When I was around your age, I went to school one day and was given a nickname.

Before I tell you the story, let me just say that some nicknames are cool. Maybe your friends have a special name for you—almost like a code word—and you smile every time you hear it. Maybe you're good at sports and everyone calls you "King James" like LeBron or "the GOAT" like Simone Biles. Or maybe you end up with a nickname you enjoy, like Garrett "the Purple Hoser" Hilbert or Cody "the Tall Guy" Jones from Dude Perfect.

But not all nicknames are created equal.

When I was in school, there was a group of cool skater kids in my grade, and I wanted them to like me more than anything. They all wore the same jeans, T-shirts, and shoes; listened to the same music; and wore their backpacks with both straps. I went to impressive lengths to be like them. I saved up money to order a skateboard and bought clothes that I could see them wearing. Their shoes were all beat up from riding skateboards, but mine were brand-new, and try as I might to kickflip and ollie to break them in, I decided to speed up the process by taking sandpaper to them to make me look legit.

I followed them around and hung out at the edges of their circle. With time they sort of accepted my presence. But I always felt like a fake; I knew I wasn't one of them.

Then one day, someone said, "Oh, look. Here comes Ratboy!"

I laughed it off, but it stung. These guys had given me a nickname, but it was the mean-spirited kind. And even though they were not being good friends to me, I still wanted to be like them—to be accepted by them, to be part of their group. Nothing about being around these people was good for me.

Over time, they introduced me to some bad habits—the kinds of things that got me into trouble and could have really put me in harm's way. And they weren't just jerks to me. They were jerks to other people, too, and I just played along as if all this cruel behavior was simply part of the deal. Being their friend mattered so much to me that I put up with it and even laughed along. If you're reading this and thinking, *Levi, you should have found some new friends*, you'd be absolutely right!

Eventually these "friends" of mine started hurting me physically too. They thought it was hilarious to kick me, sometimes so hard I passed out. After enough of these beatings, I wound up in the hospital and needed surgery. It was awful. My parents asked me what happened. And let me tell you—it's really embarrassing to have to explain to your parents and your doctor that the reason you need medical attention is because your "buddies" beat you up.

I never told any of the kids at school what had happened. I healed completely and made sure I didn't get close enough for any of them to take another kick. I moved on, but the experience scarred me—emotionally and otherwise. And now, I look back on that time and wish I could tell my younger self that fitting in just isn't worth it sometimes.

I bet you understand what it's like to want to fit in with certain people. This feeling is super normal. Everybody wants friends, and part of life is learning how to build relationships with people and choose friends who will build you up instead of tear you down. I told you that story about myself because I want you to believe that I know what you're going through. I know what it's like to feel insecure, to feel like a dork and a poser. And I know what it's like to feel left out and alone.

Since that rough time in my life, I've learned a few things that I'd like to share with you.

The doctor spun around on her little stool and clicked a few buttons on the big piece of equipment in front of Luca's eyes. Luca leaned forward, resting his chin on a little shelf, and blinked as he tried to make out the chart on the wall. Some of the letters were big; others were so tiny they looked like fuzzy little blobs.

"Luca, can you read the letters on the bottom row?" the doctor asked. "Say them out loud to me, if you can."

Luca blinked and tried to focus his eyes, but the lenses he was looking through made everything seem blurry. *Am I just nervous?* he wondered. He'd never been to an ophthalmologist before, and he didn't want to say the wrong thing and have to get glasses.

Luca's mom was sitting in the corner. "It's okay if you can't read them, honey," she said. "The doctor is just trying to help."

"I . . . I can't read them," Luca finally said.

The doctor clicked a few buttons, and the lenses in front of his eyes shifted. "Is that any better?" she asked.

Luca squinted. "I think so," he said. "But the letters are still kinda fuzzy."

She clicked the machine once more and asked Luca again. This time, he was able to read the letters aloud. "P E Z O L C," he said. "Did I get it right?"

He heard the doctor scribbling some notes on her notepad. "You did great, Luca," she said. "You can relax now." She pulled the big instrument away from his face and smiled warmly. "Why don't we all go sit in my office?"

A few weeks before, Luca had mentioned to his parents that he didn't like his seat in his homeroom class. He had been assigned a seat in the very last row, and sometimes he wished he could walk to the front of the room to see what his teacher had written on the board. Within a few days, his mother had made him an eye appointment. "You might need some glasses, honey," she had said. "My eyesight started to change a little when I was around your age."

Back in her office—where bookshelves full of heavy-looking books and large, colorful drawings of eyeballs lined the walls—the eye doctor gestured for Luca and his mom to take seats in front of her wide wooden desk. She opened his chart and cleared her throat.

"I'm glad you both came in today," she said, "because it does appear that Luca would benefit from glasses or contacts." She pushed her own glasses farther up the bridge of her nose. "Luca, I think glasses would even help you on the soccer field."

Luca could feel his face getting warm. *Glasses?!* Not many kids in his class wore glasses, and he dreaded the comments they'd make.

Registering the look of alarm on Luca's face, the doctor added, "You're

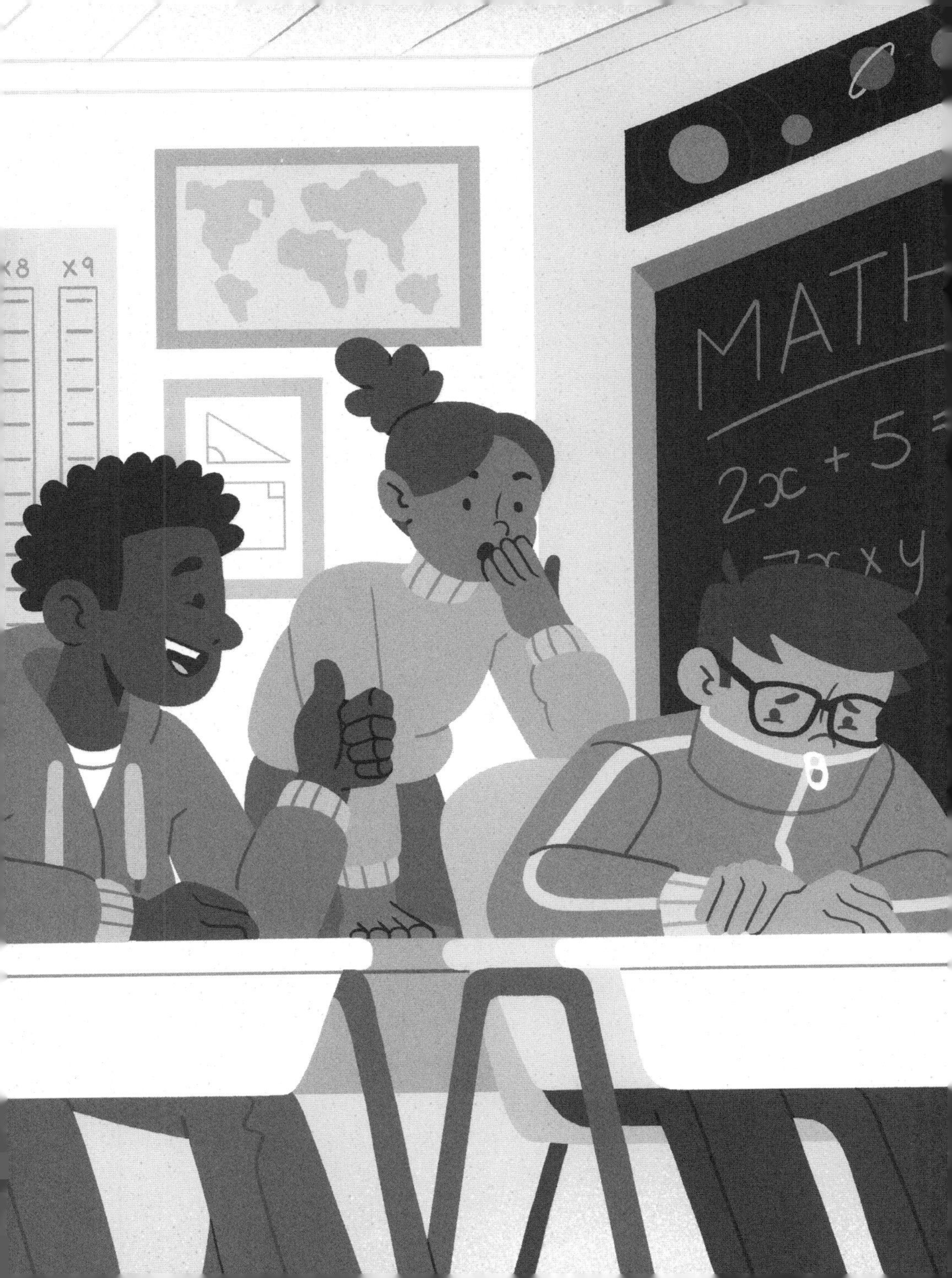
X9
2x + 5

a little young for contact lenses, but that's also an option. Mrs. Crimmins, what do you want to do?"

Luca crossed his arms and slumped down in the chair as the doctor and his mom decided his fate. He'd pick out a pair of glasses for now, and then maybe he'd try contacts in a year or so. He hated the whole situation.

Luca picked out what he considered the least horrible pair of glasses in the office. The doctor's assistant placed them over his ears and nose and tweaked them to fit him properly. As he walked out of the office, he noticed right away that everything he saw looked sharper, clearer. But he still wasn't happy.

The next morning, Luca's stomach churned as he walked into school wearing his new glasses. He had to admit that he liked being able to see so much better, but he couldn't shake the feeling that other kids were staring at him. When he walked into his homeroom, he sat down in his chair, leaned over, and pulled his jacket as far in front of his face as possible. But he could hide for only so long. When the girl who sat behind him caught a glimpse of his silver frames, she gasped.

"Ooh, Luca! When did you get glasses?"

No one said anything mean at first. Most of the kids in his class just seemed interested in this new development. "You know, Superman wears glasses when he's Clark Kent," one kid named Wriston said. "That's true," Luca said, not hating the idea of being a little like Superman.

But later that day, on the way to lunch, Luca passed another group of guys in the hall. One of them, a guy Luca recognized from soccer, pointed at Luca. "Look!" he laughed. "He's got some new faceware. What a nerd!" Luca kept on walking, unable to come up with a good comeback as the guys behind him cracked themselves up at his expense. He wanted to bury his face in a closet somewhere, but he didn't have anywhere at school to hide. He pulled up his hood again and stared at his feet, hoping no one would notice him.

When will this stupid day be over? he wondered.

Feeling like we are different can be hard—especially when all we want is to be like everybody else. As I already told you, when I was younger, I saw a group of guys at school who I thought were really cool, and I did my best to be just like them. But I faced two big problems:

1. They were not nice guys.
2. I wasn't like them at all.

Because they were bad influences and not great friends, I shouldn't have cared what they thought about me. But I did. I should have looked harder for friends who would treat me kindly and appreciate me for the person I was. But I didn't. I was insecure and had a lot to learn about myself and the kind of people I ought to surround myself with. I wish I'd known that God would give me the courage of a warrior if I would only ask.

Insecurity is a lack of confidence. It comes from uncertainty about your worth, value, or place in the world. Insecurity is believing that you aren't enough—pretty enough, rich enough, strong enough, smart enough—and that you don't have what it takes, that you aren't one of the cool kids, that the lies and harsh words people have spoken over your life are true. Does any of that sound familiar to you? Do you spend time worrying that you aren't going to be accepted by the people around you?

> **WARRIOR CHALLENGE**
>
> Lacking confidence doesn't mean you're broken. And confidence isn't something that you either have or you don't. Confidence can be *gained* and *grown* just like muscles at the gym or tricks that can be learned at the skate park. If you feel you're lacking confidence, young warrior, try this: Say one positive self-affirmation to yourself in the mirror every day. Say something like "You did a great job on your math test today!" or "You have really nice hair." Try reminding yourself that you're a warrior in training. It might sound silly, but those positive words become positive thoughts that, when repeated (like pumping a weight every day), lead to big self-confidence gains!

I get it. I still feel this way sometimes.

Fortunately, I've got a little news for you—and it's all good. Not only are you *enough* as you are, but you're also way more special than you probably know because God made you like no one else—*on purpose*.

YOU ARE ENOUGH

When we feel insecure about ourselves, we spend a lot of time trying to be something (or someone) else. We want to be cooler, more popular, smarter, richer, better looking, or maybe better at dance or sports or music. *Maybe, just maybe,* we think, *if I prove myself to be good enough, they'll accept me. They'll be my friend. They'll let me into their elite little club.*

We'll talk in a minute about why bending over backward to gain people's approval will always be a losing battle not befitting a warrior. But for now, I want you to remember one thing:

God thinks you're awesome. He thinks you're the best. And He doesn't think you have anything to prove.

Have you ever heard the song about Zacchaeus? You know, the guy who climbed a tree so he could see Jesus passing by? If you ask me, that song is brutal because most of the lyrics are about how Zacchaeus was a short dude (unlike Cody from Dude Perfect). His legacy, at least for kids who sing at church, is that he's a "wee little man"—not exactly something most people would be super proud of. Even worse, we know from the Bible that Zacchaeus was a tax collector, meaning he probably stole a lot of money from people whenever he had the opportunity. So yeah, Zacchaeus was rich—but people hated him for being a cheat.

We don't know too much else about Zacchaeus, but we do know that Jesus saw him in a tree and said, "Zacchaeus, hurry and come down! I must stay at your house today" (Luke 19:5 ICB). Zacchaeus must have felt special being singled out by Jesus, but the people around town were not impressed. "Look at the kind of man Jesus stays with. Zacchaeus is a sinner!" they said (v. 7 ICB). But Jesus cares about all of us. He decided Zacchaeus was someone He wanted to know, so He invited Himself over.

That day, Zacchaeus repented from his thieving and told Jesus he'd pay back everyone four times what he'd stolen from them. Jesus cared about the state of Zacchaeus's heart, but He certainly didn't care that Zacchaeus was a smaller-than-average type of guy. What mattered was Jesus loved him—which was more than enough. Receiving that love was enough for Zacchaeus to want to change his life for the better.

Young warrior, the next time you're feeling like you aren't good enough, remember this: You're loved by God! You don't need approval from anyone else, because the only likes that matter come from heaven—and they are already yours.

YOU ARE LIKE NO ONE ELSE

As you grow up and learn more about yourself, you'll naturally experiment with clothes and activities to see what fits you best. But have you ever found yourself mimicking the looks or behaviors of the people you want to fit in with—not necessarily because you want to be that way, but because you feel like that crowd has set the standard for how to dress and act?

Trying to be like other people can take a lot of energy until you realize you're trying to be someone you're not. Working hard to gain certain people's approval is like wearing a mask all day long. It's hot and uncomfortable inside a mask, but since it's part of a costume, you can't exactly take it off. And if you *do* take it off, everyone will see what you've been hiding.

If your only aim is to become the kind of person others approve of, how will they ever get to know the real you? And if you only try acting and dressing like other people, how will you ever figure out who *you* want to be?

As I said, being different can be hard sometimes. But have you ever thought about *why* you're different? Is it possible that God made you different *on purpose*?

God has plans and a purpose for you—and He doesn't make mistakes. When God put you on this earth, He already loved you and had given you a combination of unique qualities that no one has ever had and no one will ever have again. You are literally one in billions and billions—incredibly special beyond measure.

So why would you work so hard to be just like everyone else?

The book of Psalms is filled with a lot of praises and prayers. One such verse, Psalm 139:14, was written by King David, who specialized in writing songs for God. He sang, "I praise you because you made me in an amazing and wonderful way" (ICB). King David wasn't talking only about himself here; he was talking about every person God ever made. Each of us has been stamped with the magnificent design of our Creator—and that includes *you*. "God has made us what we are," according to Ephesians 2:10 (ICB). Special, one-of-a-kind, loved.

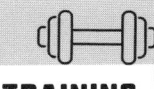

TACTICAL TRAINING

Take a moment to make a list of some gifts God has given you. If you are having trouble naming what makes you special, ask a trusted adult for help. Here are some questions to get you started.

- What can I do really well?
- What comes easily to me?
- What do I like about myself?
- What do others (my friends and family) say they like about me?
- What dreams do I have in my heart?

God didn't get stuck with you; He chose you. He's never been disgusted or surprised or shocked by anything you've done.

You are a warrior in training, and God is equipping you for good and hard adventures. So whenever you find yourself thinking, *I don't. I can't. I'm not*, respond right back: *I do. I can. I am. Because I'm loved by God!*

Though it took a couple of weeks, Luca stopped thinking so much about his glasses. At soccer practice, he wore a special pair of sports goggles with a strap around his head to keep them from falling off. And sure enough, Luca could feel that he was playing better than ever. He had a clearer view of the goalposts, and he could see his teammates waving to him across the field. Though the strap had seemed a little dorky when his dad bought it for him, he didn't care after that first practice. He liked being able to play his best, and he liked being able to see.

Back at school, no one had mentioned Luca's glasses since that first day. It was almost like he'd never had a reason to feel self-conscious at all.

Then, one afternoon in the hallway, Luca heard familiar voices behind him.

"Ooh, look who's got a metal mouth!"

"Better than those buck teeth, I guess!"

Luca turned around to see the same jerks from the soccer league who had hassled him about his glasses. This time, they were laughing and tossing another kid's lunch box around, just out of his reach. Luca knew the kid from his homeroom class—Wriston, who'd just gotten new braces.

Luca squared his shoulders and took a deep breath. Then he strode toward the bullies.

He didn't say a word at first—just snatched the lunch box out of midair and handed it back to Wriston. The two guys who'd been tossing it back and forth looked like deer caught in the headlights.

"What, did you two run out of creative insults?" Luca said, crossing his arms over his chest.

The guys tried to recover and toss out some wisecracks, but Luca didn't stick around to listen. He nodded to Wriston, and the two of them walked down the hallway in the direction of the cafeteria.

"For what it's worth, I think braces are cool," said Luca. "Maybe I'll get some, too, one day."

Wriston shrugged. "Only if you're lucky," he said. His mouth quirked up on one side as if he'd made a joke. "Anyway, thanks for helping me out, Clark Kent."

Luca laughed and pushed his glasses up the bridge of his nose. "Anytime."

GET READY FOR BATTLE

Have you ever been a victim of bullying? Maybe at school or online or even at church? Bullying is a serious issue, and you should know two things: (1) You are not alone, and (2) you have people in your life who can help you. Enlist help, young warrior. Be sure to talk to a trusted adult anytime you believe you are being mistreated. And just like Luca, do your best to stand up for others too.

STRATEGY 4

USE YOUR WORDS FOR GOOD

Have you ever been so mad you felt like you were about to explode?

It's a familiar feeling for me: My cheeks flush. My jaw clenches. I can feel my stomach tighten, and suddenly I'm balling my fists. I'm so angry that I want to hit something. I feel hurt and powerless, like I'm being treated unfairly or attacked for no good reason. I experience the all-too-familiar sensation of falling. Then, quick as a lightning bolt, mean words come pouring out of my mouth. In a flash, I think of three hundred hurtful things to say. I'm *really* mad, and I want the person I'm angry with to be sorry for what they've done to me. Maybe, deep inside, I want to hurt them too.

Can you relate?

We get mad for all kinds of reasons. Maybe you think your parents don't give you enough screen time, or they won't let you buy a video game your friends get to play. Maybe your teacher called you out in class for talking, even though you weren't the one who started the conversation. Or maybe you're mad because someone stole something from your backpack or your big brother said something rude and embarrassed you in front of your friends. When painful, unfair, or humiliating things happen, it's natural to want to lash out in response.

WARRIOR CHALLENGE

Take a moment to think about the last time you got angry about something. To get you started, here are a few questions to answer:

- Who or what made you angry?
- Describe the situation and your feelings about it. Were you hurt? Furious? Disappointed? Embarrassed?
- How did you respond to the person or situation? What did you do or say?
- How do you feel now as you think about what made you so mad?
- Do you regret your response to the situation, or was your reaction justified (or fair)?

_____

_____

_____

_____

_____

_____

Everyone gets mad sometimes—grown-ups and kids alike. Being angry is nothing to be ashamed of. In fact, we learn from the Bible that even God gets angry! When people hurt one another, He gets especially upset. But the amazing thing about God is that He is willing to forgive us when we do wrong and He shows mercy and love to all.

Young warrior, you will get angry. You probably already know the feeling well. But part of growing up is learning how to respond to your feelings of anger in healthy ways that don't hurt others and don't make you feel worse than you already do.

Every afternoon for three weeks, when she wasn't doing homework or riding her bike in the neighborhood park, Coral had been camped out at one end of the dining room table. She had heard about an art exhibit taking place at the local community center—a contest kids her age could enter. The top winner would take home a blue ribbon and a gift card to the art supply store downtown.

Coral *really* wanted that prize!

The theme for the exhibit was the animal kingdom, so Coral was building a small-scale zoo—vibrant, silly animals of all colors, fashioned out of aluminum foil, masking tape, papier-mâché, and paint. Some of the animals had googly eyes, and others were covered in glitter stripes and spots. Each animal Coral made was placed over a large landscape she had built out of cardboard, paint, and more papier-mâché. As Coral worked and added to her zoo collection, time seemed to disappear. She truly loved what she was creating.

Camila, Coral's little sister, was intensely interested in what Coral was doing. Really, Camila was interested in *everything* Coral did. But Cami could be pesky sometimes. She was only four years old, so she wasn't exactly good at helping. Whenever she tried to help Coral with her zoo animals, she mostly wound up making a huge mess.

One afternoon, while Coral was painting the finishing touches on a chubby pink-and-gray hippo with little round ears, Cami hopped up into the seat beside her. She took in the huge project in front of her, then reached for one of the glittery peacocks, knocking over the glass of water Coral used to rinse her brushes.

"Ugh, Cami!" Coral screeched, scrambling to the kitchen to find a paper towel and wipe up the spilled water. "Why do you *always* make such a mess of everything?"

Cami crossed her arms and frowned. "It was an accident." Coral huffed, annoyed that she had to deal with her sister at all. She handed Cami a paper towel and instructed her to mop up the water that had dribbled onto the floor.

"Well, you are really bad at crafts and really good at spilling stuff," Coral said.

"I just wanted to help since you don't want to play with me," Cami said, dabbing at the floor. "You never want to play with me."

Coral sighed. "I promise I'll play with you when I'm done with this. Will you just leave me alone for a while?"

Cami didn't say anything—just nodded her head and plodded back to her room. Coral finished cleaning up the spill, refilled her water glass, and went back to work.

The next afternoon, after she got off the bus, Coral's mom met her at the front door.

"Honey, there's been a little accident with your art project," Mom said, opening the door.

Coral's eyes widened. "What?" She dropped her backpack and pushed past her mother, sprinting into the dining room and taking in the damage. Glitter had been poured over every nook and cranny of her landscape, and several of the sculpted animals seemed to have been pinched and squished in the middle. Someone had poured a big glob of glue into the very center of the zoo and filled it with feathers and googly eyes. Coral's face started to get hot, and she could feel her heartbeat in her throat.

Before her mom could stop her, Coral had raced to her sister's room and thrown open the door. Cami was curled up on her bed, crying into the fluff of her favorite stuffed bunny.

"Cami, *what is wrong with you*?" she yelled.

Cami snuffled. "I . . . I—"

"Cami, you've *ruined* what I've been working on for weeks!" She moved toward the bed and got in her sister's face. "You are the most annoying sister of all time. I don't ever want to play with you again!"

"Coral, stop," Mom said, coming up behind her and pulling her away. "That's enough. She's little. She didn't mean it, and she's sorry. You have a right to be upset, but you have to remember that Cami is small and wasn't trying to hurt you. But the words you're using are *very* hurtful."

Hot tears began to pour from Coral's eyes. Who cared if her sister was sorry? The damage was done, and all Coral's hard work might as well have been flushed down the toilet. Coral stormed down the hallway to her room, slammed the door behind her, and crumpled onto the bed.

STICKS AND STONES

Sometimes when people do things that upset us, we use our words to retaliate. We want the other person to feel as bad as we feel. We want them to understand why we're mad. And sometimes we say mean words in response without thinking much about them.

But here's something we warriors need to learn as we grow up: *Even when we have good reasons to be angry, our hurtful words can do a lot of damage.*

We can all understand Coral's anger and frustration, especially if we have siblings. Younger and older siblings alike can be annoying and hard to live with, even though you love them.

Coral's mistake was not in how she felt; it was in how she responded to her feelings. Her words to Cami were unfiltered—and very hurtful. How do you think Cami felt after hearing her sister's angry words? Lonely, sad, or heartbroken? Maybe all those things?

USE YOUR WORDS FOR GOOD | 59

WARRIOR CHALLENGE

For the next few minutes, think about the last time someone said something hurtful to you. The following questions will help you think about that experience:

- What words hurt you? Who said them?
- What did those words make you feel?
- How did you feel about the person after they said those words to you? How did you respond to those hurtful words?
- How do you talk about that person to other people now? Do you tear them down or talk graciously about them?
- When did you first hear these words? How long have they been stuck in your memory?

Have you ever heard the phrase "sticks and stones may break my bones, but words will never hurt me"? I'm sure you know by now: That isn't exactly true. Words can be incredibly hurtful, and, worse than a broken bone (which eventually heals), hurtful words can stick around to hurt people for a long, long time. We can remember those words for days, months, or even years. Sometimes words are so hateful that we never forget them, even if we try. Certain insults seem to lodge themselves in our brains. And sometimes those mean words change how we think about ourselves in a harmful way.

The Bible tells us over and over that the tongue and the mouth can be dangerous if we use them to say evil or harmful words. One verse, Psalm 140:3, compares hateful words to "snake poison" (ICB). Ouch! I don't know about you, but I do *not* want a snakebite. Other verses in the Bible compare hurtful words to razors, swords, or whips—all weapons that cause people a lot of pain (Psalm 52:2, 64:3; Job 5:21). What God is trying to tell us with these comparisons is that our words matter—sometimes just as much as our actions.

> **THINK LIKE A WARRIOR**
>
> If you were bitten by a venomous snake, you would need to be given antivenom as quickly as possible. That's because the longer you wait, the less effective antivenom is at helping you get better. What about your words? If hurtful words are like snake poison, then when would be the best time to apologize for them? The longer you wait, the longer the other person feels their sting.

THREE STEPS FOR SELF-CONTROL

Sometimes we get so angry that our mouths seem to spit words out automatically. So when we're mad or frustrated, we are more likely to use words that will hurt other people. But part of growing up is learning to control your words and to *choose* not to say mean or hurtful things. This is not a simple lesson to learn, young warrior; many adults are still learning how to be kind with their words. But next time you find yourself in a situation that's really grinding your gears (old-person slang for "getting mad"), try to remember these three steps.

1. Take a deep breath (or two), then count to ten.

Maybe you've practiced this with a teacher or a parent. But even if you haven't, give it a shot on your own. Rather than "spitting fire" at someone who's upsetting you, pause. Breathe in and out slowly, then do it again. Close your eyes and count to ten. The idea is that pausing to breathe helps you calm down. Your heart and mind are connected to everything else in your body—and sometimes just taking a moment to be quiet will help that hot, angry feeling to cool down.

2. If you're still angry, leave the room for a few minutes.

Rather than saying all the hurtful things you want to say to your mom or dad or sibling or friend, go sit alone for a little while. A warrior needs time to regroup. Close your eyes and keep taking deep breaths. Maybe put on your headphones and listen to a song that you know makes you feel calm. And say a prayer to God, asking for His help and comfort. He understands why you're angry, and He understands every time you feel pain. Once you feel you have more control over the words you want to say, then you can return to the person who made you mad and talk more calmly.

3. Before you speak, remind yourself that words are powerful.

Now that you have taken a few moments to cool off, warrior, express yourself in a way that isn't cruel to the other person. Be honest about how their actions are making you feel, but do so in a way that is respectful and kind—even if they haven't shown you the same kindness or respect. This is what we call "being the bigger person"—that is, treating people well even when they don't necessarily deserve it. Being the "bigger person" is great warrior practice.

These are not easy steps. Practicing self-control is like battling with yourself; it's making hard but better choices when everything inside you would rather yell, kick, scream, or insult. But like anything we want to be good at, we get better with practice. This is a battle worth fighting, young warrior. Being able to control your anger and your words will help you be a better sibling, son or daughter, student, and friend. And it will help you feel more peace on the inside.

WORDS ARE A SUPERPOWER

You know what's funny about words? We can use them to hurt people, but we can also use them to build up people. Words kind of remind me of a superpower; depending on what you do with them, they can be used for good or evil. The villains in your favorite Marvel movies are usually the ones choosing to use their incredible strength to wreak havoc and destroy—whereas the heroes are trying to save the world, one epic battle at a time.

Here's a cool fact: Did you know that on average 16,000 words come out of your mouth per day? That adds up to a whopping 860.3 million in a lifetime. That means we have 860.3 million choices to make regarding our words: Will we warriors choose words that build up or words that tear down? I don't know about you, but I want to make sure my words are powerful in a *good* way—encouraging, positive, forgiving, loving, and kind.

Here are a few ways you can choose better words this week. Try one out and see how it makes you and others feel.

- ☐ **Compliment someone.** If you like your friend's shoes, say so. If you like what your mom made for dinner, let her know you enjoyed the food.
- ☐ **Compliment yourself.** Next time you look in the mirror, name something you like about yourself. Remember that God gave you special features—so when you appreciate something about yourself, you're also appreciating God's handiwork!
- ☐ **Thank someone.** If your bestie's mom picked you up from school and took you both to the trampoline park, don't forget to thank her. If your kid brother brought you a cold Gatorade from the fridge, high-five him and say, "Thanks, brother. You're the best." People love to feel appreciated, and gratitude will lift your spirits too.

There are many ways to use your words for good. And using words to lift up others becomes contagious. Try it with your friends or family members and see if it catches on!

Coral sat on her bed in the far corner of the room, covered in blankets. When her mom entered the room, she sat gently on the edge of Coral's bed and rested a hand on her shoulder.

"Do you want to talk about it?" Mom asked.

Coral sniffled and squeezed her eyes shut. "I'm just so mad. Why'd she do that, Mom?"

Mom sighed. "I'm not sure, honey. She might have thought she was trying to help, or maybe she was upset that you haven't been playing with her much lately. Whatever the case, I will try to find out. And I completely understand why you're upset," she said. "You know, I used to feel that way about Tía Serena too. She used to follow me everywhere, and it annoyed me so much when she would steal toys and clothes from my closet. Being a big sister can be hard."

"Did she ever wreck one of your art projects?" Coral asked.

"Not exactly," Mom said. "But she did other things that upset me. One time, she did something that made me so mad that I told her I never wanted to see her again. We were a lot older by then, but she took my words literally. We didn't see or speak to each other for some time."

Coral thought about this. "What happened?" she asked.

"Oh, just a grown-up kind of fight," her mom said. "Maybe I'll tell you more about it when you're a little older. But the point is, your sister is so little. She still has a lot to learn about what's okay and what isn't." Mom stroked Coral's arm. "I understand why you're angry. I would be too."

Coral rolled over and faced her mother. "But?"

Mom laughed. "How did you know a 'but' was coming? You're a smart cookie, my girl."

Coral felt her heartbeat slowing and her headache melting away as she looked at her mother. "But my words were hurtful, right?"

Mom nodded. "Yes, sweetie, they were. And I don't think they were true either. Cami owes you an apology, but don't you think you should pay her one too? She looks up to you so much. Anything you say to her will have a lasting impact, good or bad."

Mom was right. Coral didn't hate her sister, even though Cami annoyed her to pieces sometimes. She thought of her little sister, crying on the bed. Coral could be the bigger person this time, even though she was still hurt. The art project would still need to be repaired.

Over the next few days, Coral spent more time than she would've liked fixing all the zoo animals her sister had managed to touch. But she also did her best to fix the mess *she* had made. She apologized to Cami, told her she loved her, and said she regretted the mean words she'd said. She even made time to play in the yard with Cami and managed to incorporate some of the googly-eyed glue puddle into the final design of her handmade zoo. Overall, it wasn't *exactly* what she'd envisioned, but in some ways, it was funnier and even a little better thanks to Cami's surprise "handiwork."

All in all, Coral's hard work was enough—enough to win her first prize at the art show, that is. Coral collected her blue ribbon and spent a portion of her gift card on a little pink sketch pad for Cami. Cami's first drawing in it was simple—some colorful scribbles, crooked letters, and shapes. On the back of the page, she asked her mom to write: "To Coral. From Cami. I love you."

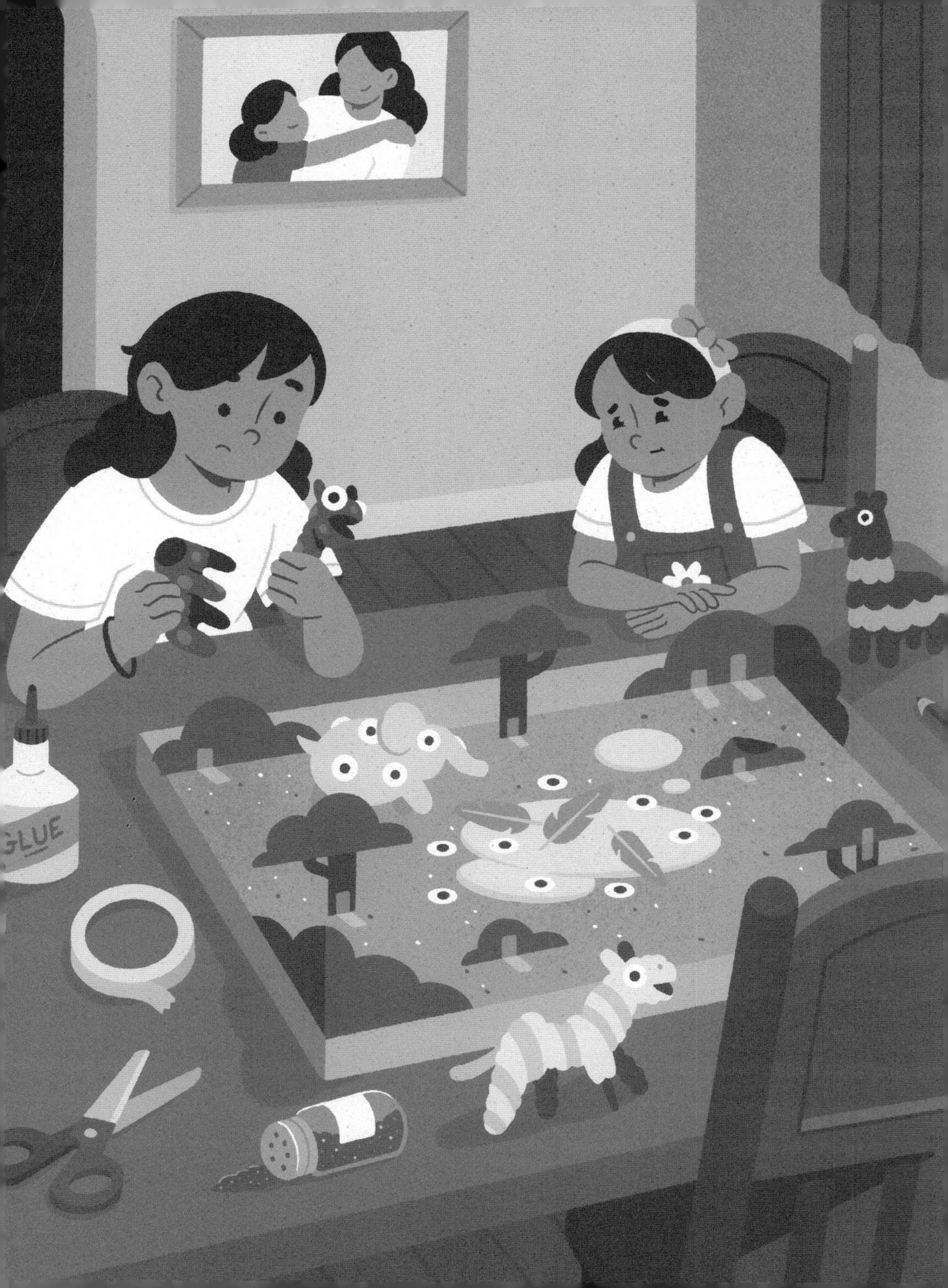
GLUE

GET READY FOR BATTLE

Think back to a situation when you said words you wish you could take back. Have you apologized yet? If not, make a plan to do that the next time you see that person. If that idea leaves you feeling scared or anxious or you're just unsure what to say, talk it out with a friend or trusted adult first. It's not easy to say you're sorry, but it's a necessary first step toward using your words for good, which is the heart of a warrior.

STRATEGY 5

LEARN TO NAME YOUR FEELINGS

Luca had been in a funk all afternoon. After lunch at school, his teacher had passed out the graded math test he'd taken the day before. Scrawled across the top of the page in thick red ink was a disappointing grade—not quite failing, but barely passing. Luca had felt frustration wash over him as he thought about how hard he'd studied for this test. *Why don't I just give up?* he wondered. *Trying isn't getting me anywhere. I should just move to another country where there isn't school.*

At soccer practice after school, he'd tried to punt his disappointment away with every practice shot at the goal. Usually soccer games and practices helped Luca forget his problems; he could run and play and focus so hard on the game that it pushed his worries to the back of his mind. But today, he couldn't shake the feeling of aggravation. Instead of focusing on the drills, his mind floated back to that ugly red mark along the top of his paper. The red scribble blew up to a hundred times its normal size in his mind's eye, and he imagined kicking the soccer ball toward it as he thwacked the ball with all his might toward the practice goal.

Does my teacher hate me? he wondered. *Is this her fault?*

No, he decided. Ms. Desmond was nice. She'd helped him so many times with math.

Did I study long enough? He thought back to the evenings he'd spent

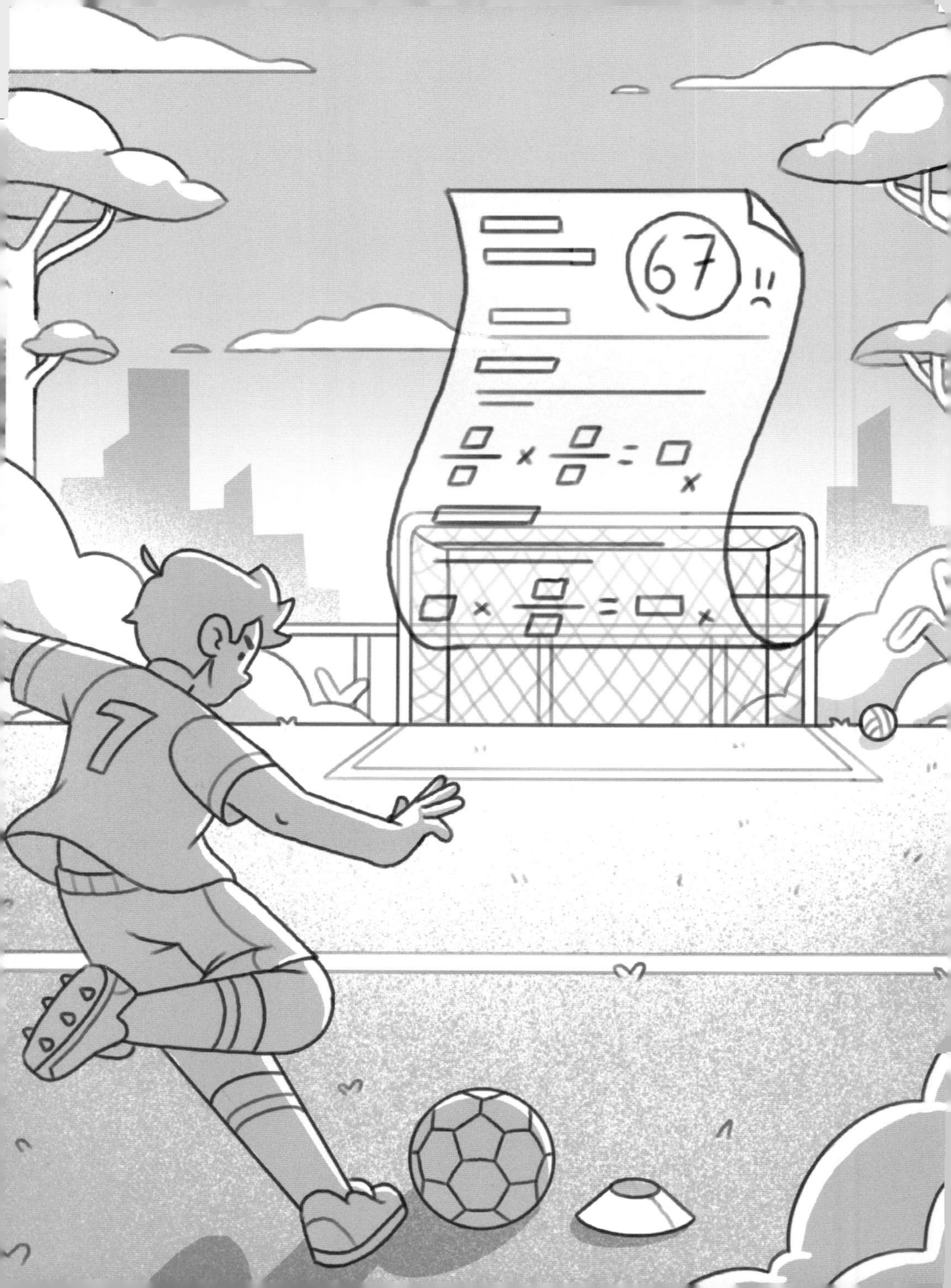
67
7

at the kitchen counter with his dad, practicing word problems and fractions and decimals. Yes, he decided, he had studied hard. And his dad had done his best to help too.

The thought that always haunted Luca knocked on the door of his brain once again.

It's because I'm dumb. I'm just bad at math because I'm dumber than everyone else. Why else would it be so much harder for me?

On the way home from soccer practice, Luca sat in the back of the minivan, stewing in his thoughts as his dad drove him home. He'd always struggled with math classes, and his parents had told him over and over that he was a smart kid who just needed to work harder at certain things. As Luca's mind spun, he focused his stare on his dad in the driver's seat in front of him. *Of course my parents have to say that*, Luca thought. *I'm their kid. What else are they going to do? Admit that I'm dumb?*

He felt his frustration building and heat rise up his neck. He crossed his arms and stared out the window. Then, he kicked the back of his dad's seat as hard as he could.

"Whoa, Chipper!" his dad said, trying to keep his eyes on the road. "What was that for?"

Luca huffed, wishing he could punch a hole in the minivan door and run home. "For being such a liar!"

Dad was silent for a second. "Um . . . what?"

"You and Mom . . ." Luca's voice began to crack, making him feel even worse. "You're liars, and you'll never admit it." With that, he gave his dad's seat two more *thunks* with his cleat.

Dad didn't say anything, but he turned on his blinker and steered the van into the vacant parking lot of a brick-red church.

"Where are you going?" Luca bellowed. "I just want to go home!"

Dad parked the car, clicked off the ignition, then opened his car door. Luca worried he might be in trouble. When Dad slid the minivan door open, he leaned an elbow on the edge of the van and looked at Luca.

"What's all this about?"

Luca just wanted to dissolve into nothing. He wasn't even sure why he had started yelling at his dad in the first place.

"Come on, Chipper. Talk to me," Dad said. He didn't seem mad at all, but Luca knew he had to answer him.

"Fine." Luca rolled his eyes as frustration and sadness morphed into something resembling rage. "I got a stupid grade on that stupid math test even though I tried my hardest. You and Mom both tell me I'm smart, but I'm *obviously* not. You're lying to me. I'm an idiot, Dad."

"Listen, Chipper. You aren't—"

"Don't call me that stupid name!"

Instead of feeling better, Luca was feeling much, much worse. Now he had yelled at his dad—turning a bad situation into a terrible one. He buried his head in his hands.

After a few silent moments, Luca felt a hand on his shoulder. "I'm going to drive us home now," Dad said. "Take some deep breaths and try to calm down. We'll talk more about this when we get home."

Luca nodded but didn't open his eyes. He did as his father said and took some slow breaths in and out. As his dad restarted the car, he began to wonder whether he had taken things too far.

How had this day managed to go from bad to worse to horrible?

MY ALTER EGO

Hello. My name is Levi, and you may remember my alter ego, Evil Levi. Evil Levi is a punk for a lot of reasons, but one of his biggest flaws is his tendency to pick fights he doesn't want to be in. Sometimes he acts like a jerk, says things that hurt people's feelings, or loses his temper and huffs around like an adult-sized toddler who hasn't gotten his way. Like I said, he's a total punk. But the real kicker is that I am Evil Levi, and Evil Levi is me. We are the same person, unfortunately.

Have you ever felt like an alien was inhabiting your body, making you do things you didn't want to do? That's how I feel when the Evil Levi part of me acts up. While deep down I know I'd rather have a fun and peaceful day and get along with my family, sometimes that ugly

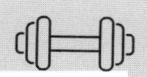

TACTICAL TRAINING

In the Hulk comics, Bruce Banner uses different coping methods like walking away or making a joke to prevent anger from, quite literally, taking over his body. Before you "Hulk out," try one of these methods for reducing your anger, frustration, or stress:

- Go for a walk or run.
- Step outside.
- Watch something funny.
- Listen to calming music.
- Take slow, deep breaths.
- Write down your feelings.
- Do something artistic.

Which of these appeals to you the most, young warrior? Have that method ready to go next time you feel your heart beginning to race and the color in your cheeks turning red . . . or green!

side of me rears up and pushes someone's buttons until they eventually poke back.

I don't want to throw tantrums. I don't want to start fights.

So why do I do it?

Here's the short answer: I flip out for a lot of reasons.

Sometimes it's because I'm feeling sensitive or uncomfortable. Or I'm feeling disrespected or like the person I'm talking to doesn't care about me. Other times I "Hulk out" because I'm feeling self-conscious or frustrated. And I have definitely thrown a tantrum or two when I felt out of control—when something didn't go my way. Fear, frustration, loneliness, confusion, sadness—these are all emotions that can encourage us to lash out at others.

USE YOUR WORDS

Maybe your mom or dad has asked you—perhaps in the middle of a conflict or difficult conversation—to "use your words." What do they mean by that? Put simply, they are asking you to think hard about your feelings and try to describe them. Some feelings are so overwhelming that they are hard to put into words—even for a warrior like you—and that's okay. Even if you try and don't feel like you're explaining yourself, that will probably be enough for your parents or guardians to better understand what you're feeling and experiencing.

The people who love you want to understand your feelings so they can help you when you need it. But using your words can also help *you* better understand why you are so sad, upset, or angry. Next time you are feeling big feelings and aren't sure why, try asking yourself these questions (or see if a family member will ask them):

- What words can I use to describe my thoughts?
- What words can I use to describe my feelings?
- What words best describe how my body feels right now?
- What happened today before I started feeling this way?
- Do I have any idea *why* I am having these feelings?

These are hard questions, and sometimes you won't know the answers. But whenever you are feeling low, moody, or downright angry, practice describing your feelings with words. Then practice talking to your parents or another trusted adult about your feelings. And don't forget: You can always talk to God.

GOD'S GOT THIS

Want to know something cool about God? You know, besides the fact that He created the whole universe without any help?

There's a book of the Bible called Proverbs, and it includes a lot of wisdom about the world. The book also has this to say about God: "The Lord looks into a person's feelings. He searches through a person's thoughts" (Proverbs 20:27 ICB). I mean, we shouldn't be *too* surprised by this, since God is all-powerful and omniscient (meaning He knows everything about everything). But it's pretty awesome to think that God knows my thoughts and feelings even better than I do.

When you find yourself having a meltdown, try saying a prayer to God. You don't have to explain yourself to Him; He already knows what you're going through. But I find that talking to God and asking for His help is a simple way to reset my spirit and regain control over my mood. Here are some situations when you might want to whisper a prayer to the God who made you:

- When you want to throw a tantrum
- When you feel like saying something mean or snarky
- When you feel like throwing a punch or kicking something
- When you want to hurt someone's feelings on purpose
- When your bad mood is all you can think about

God has a miraculous way of helping us feel better. He wants us to feel comforted and safe when we ask for His help. After all, He made you and loves you—and He loves it when you want to talk to Him.

YOU ARE IN CHARGE OF YOU

As we talked about in chapter 1, a lot of things are out of your control right now. Your training as a warrior is incomplete. Most likely, you don't get to decide where you live or where you go to school or where you attend church. Depending on your situation, you might not get to decide what to eat or wear every day either. When you're young, the adults in your life have one very important job, which is to make decisions that are good for you and keep you safe and healthy.

But as you grow older, you earn and receive more freedom; as you learn lessons about how to navigate the world, you become more able to make good decisions for yourself. One day, you'll be making *all* the decisions—which, if you ask an adult, is just *awesome* sometimes, but it can also be a lot of pressure!

I say all this to remind you that part of growing up and part of being a warrior is learning how to be in charge of yourself. Let's say it together:

You are in charge of you.

Sure, you may not get to decide what kind of ice cream your mom will buy or what you will learn in school. But here are a few important things you *can* decide for yourself:

- The words you will say (for example: say mean and false words or say nice, encouraging words)
- The actions you will take (for example: tell a lie or tell the truth; start a fight or walk away)
- The way you will treat others (for example: yell at them when you're mad or forgive them when they make mistakes; ignore newcomers or include someone who might otherwise be left out)

These may seem like small choices, but they are *really* important. The choices you make today already have consequences, as your words, actions, and treatment of others will help determine the course of your days, weeks, and years to come. Though we all make mistakes in our words and actions, we can always try to do better tomorrow. And the kinder and more patient we are with others, the kinder and more patient they will (usually) be with us.

> **WARRIOR CHALLENGE**
>
> Warriors all have a defining characteristic. Some are known for their strength; some for their speed; some for their ability to outlast the enemy, no matter how strong the attack. What's cool is that by choosing your words, actions, habits, and behaviors, you're choosing what defines you—kind of like choosing your own skills and superpowers. So decide today: In one word, how do you want to be known? Make a list of ten choices you can make to get battle-ready.

Luca was not at all excited about walking through the front door and being forced to talk to his parents. He knew he'd thrown a tantrum in the car, and he'd said disrespectful words to his dad. Was he about to be in trouble?

Dad tossed the car keys into a bowl by the front door. "Luca," he said, "drop your cleats and your bags and go sit on the couch. Mom and I will be there in a minute."

Luca did as he was told, plopping down on the couch and crossing his arms over his chest defensively.

Mom came in first and handed him a bottle of Gatorade. He searched her face for signs of trouble, but she didn't look mad.

Dad came in a moment later, and Luca's parents sat on either side of him on the couch. *Great*, he thought. *Two against one.*

"Luca," Mom started. "Why don't you tell us about what happened at school today?"

Luca chugged his Gatorade and told them about his grade on the math test. "And how did that make you feel, son?" Dad urged.

Luca felt his throat tighten. "Sad, I think. Frustrated. And it made me feel dumb."

"Honey, you're not—"

"Yes, I am," Luca interrupted. "Why else would I work so hard and still barely pass a test?"

"Luca, you're so good at so many things," Mom said, resting a hand on Luca's forearm. "Sure, math is hard. But it's hard for a lot of people. And it wouldn't be normal if you were good at *everything*—you know? No one is!"

"I was bad at math. Still am," his dad said and laughed. "Sure, I scraped by, but it never came easily to me. I had to work hard for every passing grade."

Luca had never heard his dad talk about being bad at something. Somehow, it made him feel a little better.

"What matters is you worked hard and did your best, honey," said Mom. "That's all that can be expected of anyone."

Luca felt his body relax. As his parents reminded him that he was loved, important, and good at plenty of things, he felt his anger drying up too.

"But, kiddo," Dad started, "we've gotta work on these outbursts. Sometimes when you get worked up about something, those feelings come out in weird ways. You shouldn't speak to me or your mom that way, all right? In fact, you shouldn't treat anyone that way."

Luca nodded, grateful his dad wasn't more upset. "Sorry, Dad," he mumbled.

"It's okay, Chipper. Oh, and by the way, Nana and Papa Chuck are coming over for dinner in a few minutes. Your mom invited the family over for an emergency spaghetti night."

Luca sat up straight, his eyes widening. "Really?! With garlic bread?"

His mom laughed. "Would it be spaghetti night without it? Now, go shower and put on fresh clothes before they get here. You smell just like a boy who plays soccer!"

GET READY FOR BATTLE

The last time you let your inner Hulk take over, what caused you to fall apart? Was it frustration, like Luca? Or something else—like being tired, hungry, or stressed? The goal here is to identify patterns. For example: "When I forget to eat breakfast, I typically lose my cool on the car ride to school." Who knows? Taming your alter ego—at least *some* of the time—may be as simple as stashing an extra snack (or two) in your bag.

Being able to identify (name) your feelings is the first step to having control over them. Don't let those outbursts get the best of you, young warrior. You are stronger and smarter than they are!

STRATEGY 6

CREATE GOOD HABITS

The leaves outside Coral's window had all turned to dappled colors of red, brown, and orange. One tree—Coral's *favorite* tree—sported bright yellow leaves with green spots and was rustling in the autumn wind. Though Coral still missed her family and her home back in Texas, she had to admit that her new home and city was pretty in the fall.

"Coral! We leave in five minutes!"

Mom and Dad were hustling around the house, trying to get everyone ready for Sunday morning church. Coral's big brother, Matteo, seemed to always want to stay in bed in the mornings, both on Sundays and every other day too. Coral figured he'd sleep all day if their parents let him. Cami, on the other hand, woke up at the crack of dawn, but she had no sense of order or direction. Some days it took the whole family to get Cami dressed because she had the energy of a rubber bouncy ball.

Coral was dressed and ready to go, and she'd already eaten her breakfast. So she turned off the light in her bedroom, headed downstairs, and climbed into the car before anyone else. As Mom buckled Cami into her safety seat, she looked up and winked at Coral. "Thank you for getting yourself ready today," she said. "When you do that, you're a big help to me."

Coral felt warm inside. She liked being helpful, and she liked being able to take care of herself. It was one of her favorite parts about getting older.

The church they attended wasn't too far from home, so they pulled around the red-brick building and into the busy parking lot a few minutes later. As soon as Coral hopped out of the car, she spotted Millie, her friend from school, and gave her a wave.

"Hi, Millie!"

"Hi, Coral!"

The two girls made their way inside and headed straight to their youth group. Coral had enjoyed attending this church since her family first moved to town. So far she'd made several friends, some of whom went to her school. She liked her Sunday school teachers, and during the bigger service, she sometimes got to sit with her friends. Coral didn't even have too many complaints about the sermon, the long speech that happened in the middle of the service. She liked the way she felt when everyone sang together during the worship time, and recently, she'd tried praying along and sharing her thoughts with God.

After church was over and the adults were milling about, Coral's friend Millie rushed over to her.

"I forgot to ask you earlier! What are you doing for the science project?"

Coral furrowed her brow at first, then her eyes widened in recognition. "I . . . um . . . uh—"

"My dad and I built some rockets together," Millie interjected. "We set them off and then measured how far away they flew from the takeoff location. It was so fun! I'd never built a rocket before—have you?"

Coral hadn't, but she was too wrapped up in her thoughts to answer. As Millie kept talking, her voice seemed to get quieter and quieter as Coral's mind raced. She had messed up, she realized. She had messed up in a big way.

She interrupted Millie's chatter and said, "That's due . . . tomorrow, right?"

"Yep, tomorrow. I've been working on it for, like, three weeks. I hope I get a good grade." Millie's eyes caught something behind Coral. "Oops, my mom's waving at me. Time to go. Bye, Coral!"

Coral remained frozen in place as Millie bounced off with her family. Coral's stomach started to feel like a blender as reality sank in: Her big science project—the one assigned on one of the first days of school—was due *tomorrow*. And she hadn't even started it yet.

As they usually did on Sundays, Coral's family went out to brunch after church. Today they had chosen a new spot they had never tried before, and Coral ordered banana pancakes with syrup and bacon—one of her all-time favorite dishes. But as everyone around her gobbled down their lunch, Coral could barely touch her plate. She stared at the golden pancakes, dripping with butter and maple syrup. Her appetite seemed to have vanished.

"Honey," said Dad, "is something wrong with your lunch?" He pointed a fork at her full plate.

"You've been awful quiet since we left church," Mom said.

"Awful quiet," Cami said, shaking her head. She was doing even more of that than usual these days—repeating whatever anyone else said first.

"Well, I, uh . . ." Coral hated being put on the spot. She needed to fess up about the science project, but she hated that everyone's eyes were on her.

"Just spit it out already!" Matteo said around a mouthful of food.

"Fine!" Coral huffed. "I have a huge science project due tomorrow. I kinda forgot about it, but I also kinda put it off. And now I'm out of time, and I don't even have an idea for what kind of experiment to do, and I'm gonna fail science because of this, and I have no idea what to do about it, all right?" Having told the whole, ugly truth, she covered her face with her hands and plopped her elbows on the table.

The whole family paused a moment to take it all in, looking around at one another as their thoughts processed. "So let me get this straight," Dad said, taking another sip of coffee. "You have a big project due tomorrow, and you haven't even *started*?"

Coral nodded, her hands still covering her face.

Mom pinched the bridge of her nose, then let out the longest, most exhausted sigh that had ever been sighed. "Coral, we've been through this before. Why did you wait so long to start a project you knew was going to take you a long time?"

"I don't know," Coral said, exasperated by the situation, but mostly by herself. "I didn't want to do it right away, and I guess I just forgot about it. I probably wouldn't have remembered it at all if Millie hadn't mentioned it."

Coral's parents shared a look—the kind parents share when they are irritated by their kids. Then her dad made a swirling motion with his hand as if twirling a lasso.

"All right, everybody, let's wrap up this brunch. We gotta get home and help Coral invent a science project out of thin air."

"Out of thin air," little Cami said, twirling her own imaginary lasso.

As Coral packed her barely touched pancakes in a to-go box, she said a little prayer, thanking God for helpful parents. She also asked for a little inspiration regarding her project—as she had *no idea* where to start.

BEWARE YOUR (BAD) HABITS

When you hear the word *habit*, what comes to mind? Odds are, you've learned quite a bit in your life about good and bad habits. But in case you need a quick refresher, a *habit* is a pattern of behavior—meaning it's something you do regularly.

Here are some examples of good habits. These routines are helpful because they keep your home and your body clean:

- brushing your teeth before bed
- putting your dirty clothes in the hamper
- taking dirty shoes off at the door
- placing your dinner plate in the sink or dishwasher
- hanging your wet towel after a bath or shower

But we can pick up bad habits, usually without trying to, like these:

- being late (tardy) to school or practice
- leaving trash on the seat or floor of the car
- hitting the snooze button on your alarm too many times and showing up late as a result
- using bad language
- looking at things on your devices that you know you shouldn't
- neglecting to say "thank you" or "please" when appropriate

Do you recognize yourself in any of these habits, good or bad?

TACTICAL TRAINING

Take a few minutes to make a list of your daily routines, as well as lists of your good and bad habits. Some of the good habits you practice may be inspired by rules you are expected to follow at home or in school. But be honest and list your bad habits too. What behaviors—maybe negative habits—tend to get you in trouble?

My Routines

_____
_____
_____
_____

My Good Habits

_____
_____
_____
_____

My Bad Habits

_____
_____
_____
_____

If you find yourself looking at a long list of bad habits, welcome to the club!

Habits are hard to break because they're things we do all the time—so often, in fact, we tend to do them automatically.

Try to remember the last time you placed your cup of water on the coffee table, your desk, or even the carpet in front of the TV. Did you remember to take it to the sink when you were done, or did you move on without even *thinking* about your cup again? You didn't necessarily leave it there on purpose; you were just thinking about other things. You forgot it. You moved on.

Maybe you leave your cup on the floor so often that someone inevitably kicks it over and makes a mess. Or maybe your dad is tired of picking up after you, so he fusses at you to "Put away this cup!" every time he sees one lying around. Either way, you're a young warrior with a bad habit. And it would probably be great for everyone if you learned to clean up after yourself and kick that habit to the curb.

Habits are often things we do automatically—steps we take without thinking. That's why bad habits are so hard to break! To change our behavior, we have to first *notice* our behavior, then actively try to *change* it.

OUR CHOICES MAKE US

Some bad habits are symptoms of our laziness. To keep this cup of water metaphor going—maybe you actually *decide* to leave your cup on the floor. You know you shouldn't, but you do it anyway because you don't want to make the trip to the kitchen sink. In this case, you've made a choice.

And here's the thing about choices: *Little by little we make our choices, and then our choices make us.*

What do I mean by that?

Every little choice we make each day determines who we are and what we become. As we've already discussed, some choices aren't yours to make yet—but plenty of choices *are*. Your thoughts, your words, how you respond to your moods, what feelings you act on, how you talk to your parents and friends, the way you treat those in authority, and how you speak to yourself are all like drips of water. And what happens when enough water drips on a rock?

Over time, many drops of water can carve a groove in a jagged rock.

Then enough drops of water slide down that groove and combine to become a creek.

More and more drops combine, and the creek becomes a river.

Given enough time, many drops of water—multiplied enough times—can eventually create the Grand Canyon. And it all started with a single drop. And your good habits all start with a single good choice.

THE KIND OF WARRIOR YOU WANT TO BE

We could talk all day about the importance of good habits. But how, you may be wondering, can you begin developing *better* habits? This is a skill you will practice your entire life, young warrior. But for today, here are three steps for you to try.

Step 1: Decide on a good habit you'd like to build.

Spend a few minutes with a parent or guardian looking over the lists you just made about your routines and your habits. Can you think of a good habit you would like to practice—something that would make your life easier, better, or more exciting? Together, try to name at least one new good habit you would like to cultivate.

Step 2: Make a battle plan.

Talk to your trusted adult about how they can help you implement this new habit into your life, and write down a few practical ideas for how you will make it happen on your end. For example, if your goal is to keep your room tidier, designate a time each week (or even every few days) for picking up and cleaning. Have your parents write down the times on a calendar and ask them to remind you when it's time to clean.

Step 3: Set a goal and stick to your guns.

Good habits don't usually form themselves; instead, like any other skill, they're practiced and honed. Once you've chosen a habit to cultivate and made a plan of action, set a goal for yourself to repeat that action several times in a row. If you only clean your room once, you haven't formed a habit. But if you clean your room twice a week for two months, the routine starts to feel automatic. Write down your goal—for example, "I want to clean my room twice a week every week until my birthday"—then, for some positive reinforcement, talk to your parents about a reward system that could encourage you to meet your goal.

Believe it or not, you are already well on your way to becoming the person—the warrior—you will be for the rest of your life. Yes, you will change a lot during your lifetime, but my point is that the habits you build today have the potential to stick with you for a long, long time. Those habits can be good, or they can be bad.

You also have the option *today* to declare war on the bad habits you've already developed, and with God's help, young warrior, you are *more than able* to defeat them!

THE PRODIGAL SON

One of Jesus' best-known parables is about a young man who grew up and decided to leave his family behind. The young man asked his father to give him everything he was set to inherit—a very rude thing to do, by the way—then went off to do whatever he pleased. We can imagine that this choice hurt the young man's family deeply—especially his father.

Here's what the Bible says the young man did next:

> He traveled far away to another country. There he wasted his money in foolish living. He spent everything that he had. Soon after that, the land became very dry, and there was no rain. There was not enough food to eat anywhere in the country. The son was hungry and needed money. So he got a job with one of the citizens there. The man sent the son into the fields to feed pigs. The son was so hungry that he was willing to eat the food the pigs were eating. But no one gave him anything. (Luke 15:13–16 ICB)

I don't know about you, but the idea of eating pig slop is *super* gross to me. Do you think the son was regretting his choices at this point?

We don't know anything about the kind of person this young man was before he left his father's house. Maybe he was an obedient son who cleaned his room regularly and brushed his teeth three times a day.

But I doubt it.

The son's choice to leave home was probably one of many bad decisions. His choice to leave implies he was not happy at home and wanted to see what else the world had to offer. Maybe he and his brother didn't get along. Or maybe he didn't want to follow the house rules anymore. Whatever the case, he must have hurt everyone by running away. Soon, though, he discovered his father's house wasn't so bad after all.

Want to know what happened next?

> The son realized that he had been very foolish. He thought, "All of my father's servants have plenty of food. But I am here, almost dying with hunger. I will leave and return to my father. I'll say to him: Father, I have sinned against God and against you. I am not good enough to be called your son. But let me be like one of your servants." So the son left and went to his father. (Luke 15:17–20 ICB)

What do you think the son expected to happen when he returned home? Do you think he assumed he'd be punished for running away and wasting all his father's money? What he found at his father's house must have been a huge surprise:

> While the son was still a long way off, his father saw him coming. He felt sorry for his son. So the father ran to him, and hugged and kissed him. The son said, "Father, I have sinned against God and against you. I am not good enough to be called your son." But the father said to his servants, "Hurry! Bring the best clothes and put them on him. Also, put a ring on his finger and sandals on his feet. And get our fat calf and kill it. Then we can have a feast and celebrate! My son was dead, but now he is alive again! He was lost, but now he is found!" So they began to celebrate. (Luke 15:20–24 ICB)

That's right—they had a *party*. Instead of being furious, the dad gave his son a bear hug and said, "Wahoo! You finally came home! Somebody call Domino's and order a hundred pizzas!" (Okay, not really. They killed the family's fattened calf and made a feast.)

Many people love this story because the father is supposed to remind us of God. God loves His children and forgives them every day, no matter what they've done wrong. How wonderful to know that God—the Creator of the whole, wide, breathtaking, infinite, beautiful universe—loves us enough to call us His family!

We also learn from the son in this story that it's never too late for us to change for the better. The son made some of the worst mistakes a person can make—yet he turned his life completely around. He recognized that he needed help and his choices had not been good, but the moment he decided to make better decisions, his father threw open the door and waved him back inside.

WARRIOR CHALLENGE

Have you heard the word *repentance* before? It's a Bible term that Jesus used often in His preaching (see examples below). Your Bible might use the phrase "change your hearts" instead. And that's what repentance means: making a change so drastic it's like a 180-degree turn. Look up the following verses and discuss with a trusted adult why you think this message was so important to Jesus.

+ Matthew 4:17
+ Luke 5:32
+ Luke 13:3, 5

We make mistakes too—big and small. Some of those mistakes become habits. But even with bad habits, we can make choices to turn our lives around. This is part of growing up and maturing as a warrior. We *choose* behaviors that are respectful to others, to God, and to ourselves. Good habits will make us more pleasant to be around and often make us feel better too. And don't forget: What you choose today lays the groundwork for the kind of person you will become.

Back at home, Coral stared at the piece of paper outlining the directions for her science assignment. Her panic continued to rise as she realized this was *not* something she could throw together last minute. She should have started days ago, even *weeks* ago. But once again, she had put it off and forgotten.

Coral's dad sat beside her at the dining room table, then took the piece of paper from her hands. He perched his glasses on his nose to read the instructions for himself.

"Not good, Coral," he said, laying the paper down on the table. "I can help you get organized today, but I don't see how you could finish this by tomorrow."

Coral's shoulders slumped. She knew her dad was right. "Should I even bother at this point? What should I do?"

Mom stepped into the room and leaned against the doorframe. "I think you should start and spend as much time on it as you can today. Then, tonight before bed, we should sit down and write an email to Mrs. Patel explaining how you're behind on your work and why. She may be willing to give you some extra time, but she may not. Either way, she should be made aware of the situation."

Coral nodded. "Okay," she said. "But what should I do right now?"

"Flip through your notes and your textbook for ideas," said Dad. "Starting is the hardest part, but try to channel that creative part of you. I bet you can come up with something."

For the rest of the afternoon, Coral researched project ideas. She eventually landed on one that interested her and wouldn't require many materials. Because she loved watching things grow, she decided to compare types of seeds and how quickly they germinate—but it would take a few days, at least, to record her findings.

After dinner and another hour of setting up her project, Coral joined her mother on the couch and typed an email to Mrs. Patel. She wrote that she was sorry, that she was behind on her work, and that she would bring her completed project to class as soon as possible. Then she pressed Send.

Mom turned to her. "Coral, this isn't the first time this has happened. We need to figure out why this is your habit."

"I'm not totally sure, Mom. I think, at first, I put it off because . . . I just didn't want to do it. But eventually I forgot about it." She let out a long sigh.

"Well," Mom said, "I think we need to come up with a system of organizing your assignments. Then change some of your homework habits so this doesn't happen again."

The next morning at school, Mrs. Patel asked Coral to chat with her

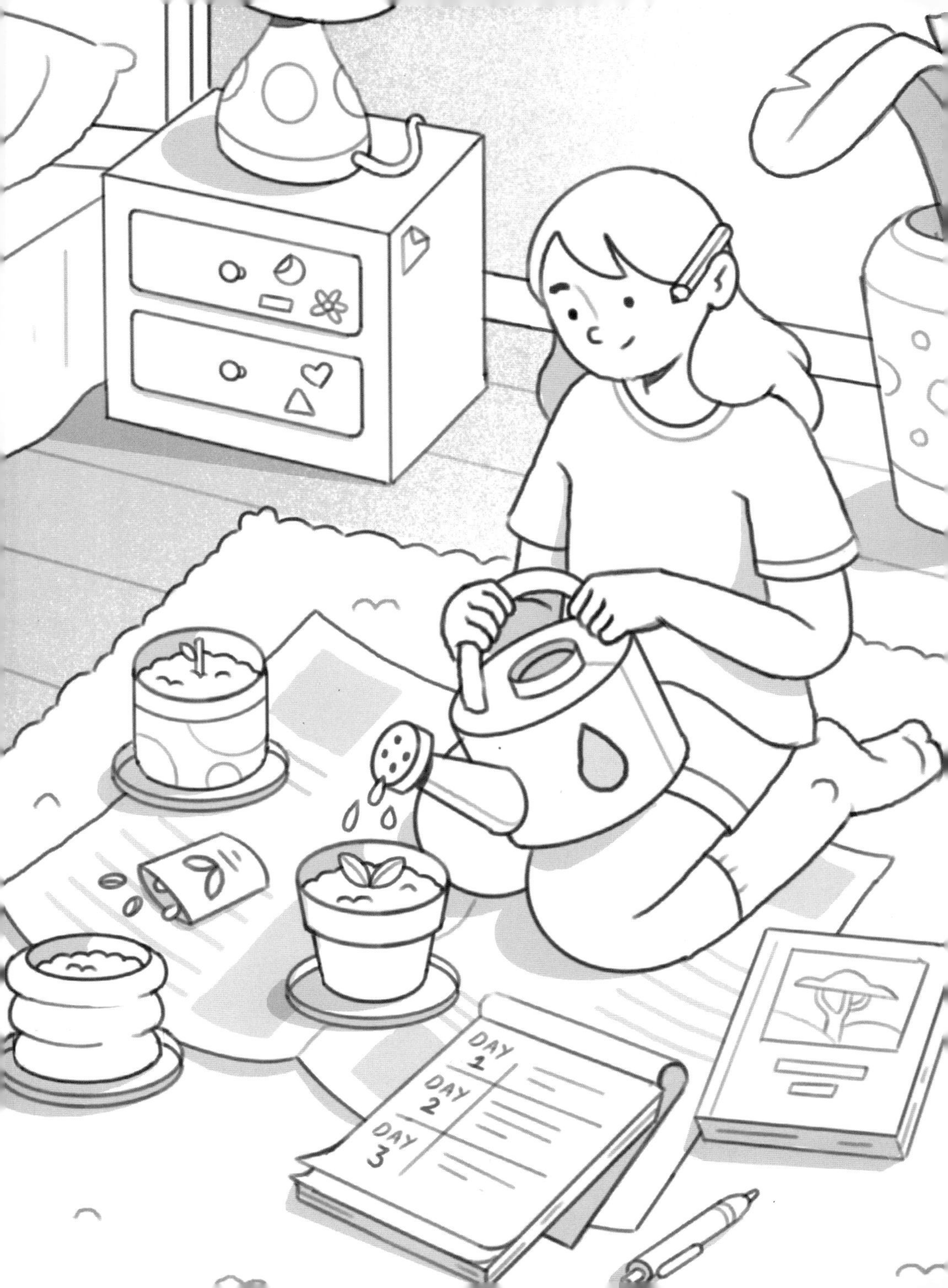
DAY 1
DAY 2
DAY 3

about the science project. "Thank you for emailing me," she said. "I'm afraid you'll lose a little credit for turning it in late, but I'm happy you chose to start it when you did. Let me know if I can help you with it, okay?"

Coral was grateful Mrs. Patel wasn't angry and that she wouldn't be penalized too harshly. Back at home after school, she ran to her bedroom and checked on her little seeds to see if any of them had sprouted. One of them already had!

After dinner, she and her parents sat down at the dining room table and tried to organize her assignments for the rest of the month. For the longer projects that needed more time and attention, they made a plan to break the work into little bits each day.

"One day soon, you should be able to organize your work all on your own," Mom said. "But for now, your dad and I are here to help. No more procrastinating, okay?"

All Coral had to do was stick to the plan they had made—and she decided right then and there that she would.

GET READY FOR BATTLE

Feeling overwhelmed isn't the only reason we put things off. What about procrastinating simply because you're bored by the activity? It's okay not to want to do something—but instead of complaining about it or avoiding it, make it fun! Get creative, young warrior! Set a timer when you fold laundry and try to beat your previous record. Play music and dance while you pick up your room. Think of more ways to *fun*-ify your least favorite activities!

STRATEGY 7

CHOOSE TO BE BRAVE

Hey, warrior. Let's try a little game as we start this chapter together. Grab a sheet of paper—either construction paper, notebook paper, or something you can snatch from the printer tray.

Got it?

Great. Now take your piece of paper and fold it in half.

Now fold it in half again.

Still got it?

Cool, let's do it again.

And again.

I bet your paper has gotten a lot smaller by now! But see if you can fold it again.

And again.

And again.

Wait—what did you say? You can't fold it anymore? Why not?

Here's a fun fact for you: If you attempt to fold a single sheet of paper in half multiple times, you won't be able to fold it more than seven or eight times. The TV show *MythBusters* proved that you can go as high as eleven, but their paper was the size of a football field, and they used a forklift and steamroller to fold it inside Kennedy Space Center, so I'm not sure it counts.[1] The world record number of folds stands at twelve, accomplished by a teenager who used toilet paper for the experiment.[2]

So, yeah. Your piece of paper was *never* going to fold ten times or more. It's basically scientifically impossible! If you want, try it with other kinds of paper to see if your results vary—but my guess is you'll be able to fold it fewer than seven times, each time.

Folding paper shows the power of *compounding*—a term you might remember from math class. In the case of your paper experiment, every time you fold the page, it doubles in thickness. First you have one page, but after folding you have two; a fourth fold makes sixteen pages, and on it goes, doubling and doubling and doubling. If you could keep up this progression, by the time you got to twenty-three folds, your stack of pages would be a kilometer, or 3,280.84 feet, high.

Thirty folds? It would reach higher than three hundred thousand feet into the sky—the beginning of outer space.

Forty-two folds? To the moon.

Fifty-one? Your stack of paper is now on fire, because it has reached the sun.

And if you could somehow hit 103 folds, the stack that started as a single sheet of paper would measure 93 billion light-years from end to end, stretching across the boundaries of the known universe.

Those are some wild calculations, right? And they all started with *one*.

I'm sharing these numbers to prove a point about how things multiply—specifically, our choices and behaviors. In the last chapter we talked about building better habits and how *choosing* good words and actions is the first step toward taking your life in a new direction. But what if you *continue* taking steps in that direction? Eventually, you will travel a block, then a mile. And if you keep on walking, you will eventually wind up in another state or country!

Think about your favorite musician, athlete, artist, or gamer. Do you think they just tried something once and became experts overnight? No way! Everyone who's great at something *practices* what they do—and their greatness compounds from the first time they try their craft to every time after. *But greatness always starts with a first try.*

PRACTICE REQUIRES COURAGE

What you're doing now matters. Your choices today will build on your choices from yesterday, and every day will present new opportunities for you to practice making better choices, standing up for what's right, and being your best self.

But those choices will not always be easy.

Think back to that favorite musician. At some point, he ran into a day (probably many days!) when it was hard to get to the recording studio. Maybe he felt sick or tired or wasn't in the mood. Maybe he had trouble with a song and spent three weeks trying to nail down the ending. Eventually, because he kept trying and didn't give up, we got to enjoy his hit record. He kept practicing even when it was difficult.

It's important to keep making good decisions even when it's hard.

It's one thing to "not feel it" or to run into struggles creatively. But what about something being hard because you're being pressured to do something you know is not right? Or when you have the opportunity to make something easier by cheating, stealing, or lying without getting caught? Choosing to do the right thing in circumstances like that requires more than commitment—it requires warrior-level courage, inner strength, and a whole lotta guts.

The afternoon was Luca's favorite time of each weekday. He'd head home after school, change into his soccer gear, gobble down a snack, chug a Gatorade, and ride over to the field for practice. As the fall days grew shorter and cooler, Luca enjoyed the practices even more. The crisp air cooled his neck as he sprinted up and down the field, chasing the ball and running drills with his team.

Some older boys from the league also played on his team, and he'd made friends with some of them this season. Being with the older guys made Luca feel more mature, and he liked that they treated him as an equal.

One afternoon, a few of the guys were waiting for their rides after a long, tiring practice. Luca's dad was running late, so Luca was standing around when two of the older players, Dylan and Finn, waved him over.

"Luca, you've got to see this," Dylan said. He and Finn were huddled together, laughing over something on a cell phone. Once Luca got closer, Dylan flashed him the screen.

Luca's face grew hot at what he saw.

Luca had talked several times with his parents about getting a cell phone, but they had decided he was too young. His parents had also warned him about situations like this, where he might be around other kids who *did* have them.

"Want to see more?" Dylan asked. "There are like a million more pictures."

Luca wasn't completely sure what he was looking at—but he knew it was something he probably shouldn't be seeing. His brain seemed to shut down a little, and he felt like his feet were glued to the pavement.

"I . . . uh . . ." he stammered.

"Check this one out," Finn said, taking the phone out of Dylan's hand and scrolling through images. He turned the screen back toward Luca.

"Nah, I'm good," Luca said, finally finding his voice. He held out a hand and took a couple of steps backward, the heat still spreading along his neck and into his cheeks.

"Uh-oh, our wittle buddy Luca's being a wittle bitty baby," Dylan teased, dragging out the words in a way that made Luca feel horrible. Finn cackled and went back to scrolling.

"I'm not a baby," Luca said, struggling to find the right words. "I just . . . don't wanna . . ."

"I don't wanna!" Dylan mocked, using his best baby voice. "Man, Finn, how did we get stuck on a team with babies?"

Luca hated being called a baby, but being called a baby by his teammates? He felt about an inch tall. These guys were supposed to be his friends—they shouldn't be turning on him like this.

He suddenly felt sick.

If he went along, tried to play it cool, would they take it back? Luca wondered.

He took a step forward.

But just as Luca was about to say something more, his dad pulled up in their minivan and honked the horn twice. Luca's head swiveled in the direction of the vehicle, and Dad rolled down his window.

"Sorry, Chipper," he said, using Luca's nickname. "Got a little held up in a meeting this afternoon. Let's go."

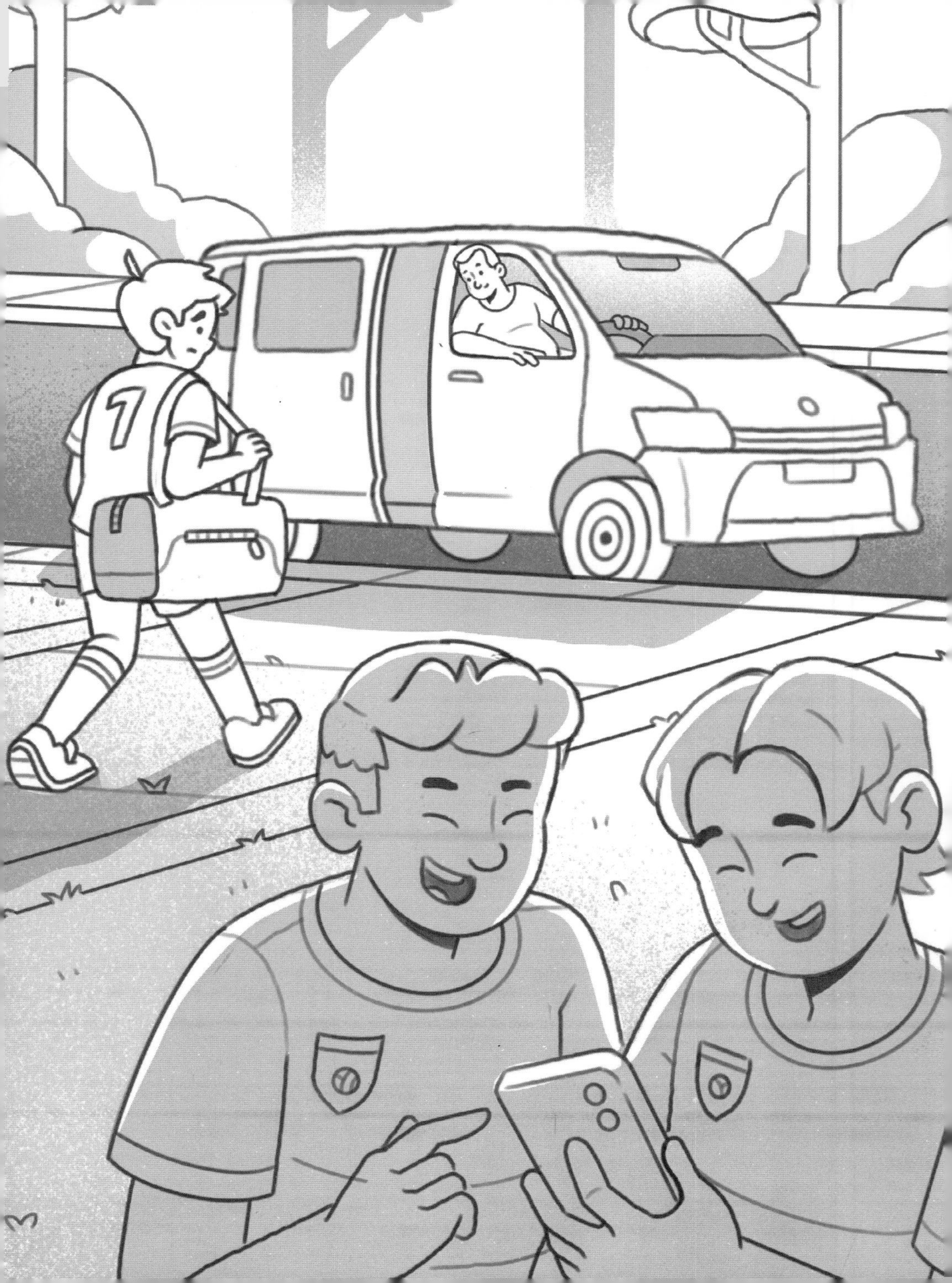
7

Luca said bye to Dylan and Finn as he shouldered his duffel bag, but they didn't respond, heads still poised over the cell phone. As Luca opened the van door, though, he heard a voice call out behind him:

"Yeah, bye, loser." Then two voices laughed loudly.

Luca tossed his bag into the van, slumped down in his seat, and slammed the door shut. All the way home, he felt like he'd been punched in the gut.

Luca was sullen and quiet for the rest of the evening. He didn't want to be in a bad mood, but the words of his teammates kept swirling in his head. Though he knew Finn and Dylan were looking at pictures they shouldn't have, he had been *very* close to caving and joining them too. *What if I had?* Luca wondered. *Would they have still called me a baby and a loser?*

Once he and his dad had gotten home, they'd been greeted by Nana and Papa Chuck. Nana had come over to cook with Mom, and they had made one of Luca's favorites—a big bowl of pasta carbonara.

"Extra cheesy for my Luca," Nana had said, winking as she set his plate in front of him at the dinner table.

As he spun his fork through the creamy noodles, Luca tried to push the afternoon out of his mind. But he must have looked distracted anyway.

"What's on your mind, Chipper?" Papa Chuck asked. "You seem a bit low tonight."

Luca shrugged. "Nothing, really." He kept his eyes on his plate, not wanting to talk about the day during dinner. The whole thing felt too embarrassing for words.

After the dishes were washed and homework was done, Luca climbed into bed. He propped himself up against a pillow reading *Superman: The Man of Steel*. The Superman comics were his favorite—especially since he'd acquired his own Clark Kent glasses.

He heard a light knock, and Papa Chuck cracked open the bedroom door.

"Can I come say good night, Chipper?"

Luca nodded and set down his comic. Then Papa Chuck made room for himself on the side of Luca's bed.

"You seem down today, Chipper," he said. "Everything okay?"

Luca frowned. He didn't want to lie to his grandfather, but he didn't want to talk about what had happened either.

"You can trust me," Papa Chuck said, his eyes twinkling. "Don't forget you're the chip off my old block, after all."

The side of Luca's mouth quirked up in a grin. His grandfather had been the one to give him his nickname—so long ago he didn't even remember it happening. In Luca's heart, he had always been Chipper, and since he loved his grandfather, he loved the nickname too.

Luca sighed, gearing up to tell the truth. "I . . . um . . . well, I saw something today I shouldn't have."

Papa Chuck listened quietly as Luca recounted the afternoon—Dylan, Finn, the cell phone, and the way they'd laughed at him. Luca even confessed that he'd been tempted to look, if only to get them to stop calling him names.

Papa Chuck took a long, deep breath and then released it. "Well, Chipper, sounds like you did something brave today."

Luca looked up. "I did?"

"Sure you did! You felt in your gut you weren't supposed to look at that phone, and you followed that gut instinct by saying no. Standing up to bullies like that takes courage. And I can tell you those guys are wrong about you because losers aren't brave at all." Papa Chuck reached over and gave Luca's shoulder a squeeze.

"I'm afraid you'll probably experience more situations like that in the future, Chipper," Papa Chuck continued. "But bravery is like a muscle. The more you use it, the stronger it gets. I've got a feeling you're only going to get braver and braver. I'm proud of you, kid."

Papa Chuck asked Luca to show him a couple of pages of the comic book before giving him a bear hug and a kiss on the head. He asked permission to tell Luca's dad about what happened, and Luca gave it. It would save him another awkward conversation that way.

That night, as Luca rested his head on his pillow and closed his eyes, he felt safe. And his heart felt warm and full.

YOU CAN BE BRAVE

When you think about the word *brave*, maybe you're like me (and Luca) and tend to think about superheroes: strong characters—warriors—fighting epic battles and vanquishing scary villains using their superhuman skills and strength.

But bravery is found in all kinds of places, in all kinds of people. And you, warrior, can be every bit as brave as you want to be.

TACTICAL TRAINING

Do you have someone in your life like Papa Chuck? An adult you trust and can talk to openly? If so, this is probably someone you look up to—someone with impressive qualities you'd like to learn from and imitate. But get this: This person has qualities he or she admires about you too! Next time you see them, ask these questions: What are my strengths? What are my best qualities? You might be surprised to learn all the ways you're *already* setting an example for those around you.

In the Bible, we read about a young guy named Timothy who did some great things for God. We know Timothy was young because these words were written to him from his teacher, Paul: "You are young, but do not let anyone treat you as if you were not important. Be an example to show the believers how they should live. Show them with your words, with the way you live, with your love, with your faith, and with your pure life" (1 Timothy 4:12 ICB).

How awesome is that? I mean, that verse is about *you*. God has always known that young people can be not only brave but also examples of bravery. You can fight for good things with courage and strength. Even more, you can be a role model—to people younger *and* older than you!

Maybe that feels like a lot of responsibility, but it should also feel good to know that God believes you have what it takes to act bravely when given the opportunity. And every time you choose to act with courage, you will notice that it only gets easier and easier.

THE KID WHO WAS A KING

Speaking of young people in the Bible, did you know one of Israel's very best kings was a kid? His name was Josiah, and he was eight years old when he became ruler of the nation (2 Kings 22:1). Many kings before and after him made decisions that dishonored God, but Scripture tells us that Josiah "did good things as his ancestor David had done" and "did not stop doing what was right" (v. 2 ICB). David, as you may know, was also a young warrior during his time, having defeated Goliath the giant—a supersized villain if there ever was one—with a slingshot, a stone, and his faith in God's protection (1 Samuel 17). He, too, became a king and ruled over Israel with the help of God.

Both these young heroes made brave choices and stood firm in their obedience. Never once did

THINK LIKE A WARRIOR

Goliath was the champion fighter of the Philistines. The Bible says his armor alone weighed approximately 125 pounds—that's like trying to carry three giant bags of dog food all at the same time!

Goliath was really, *really* tall too. How tall do you think he was?

a. Six feet, nine inches tall
b. Seven feet, six inches tall
c. Eight feet, ten inches tall
d. Nine feet, four inches tall

Answer: D! Some sources even say he was a few inches taller: nine feet, nine inches tall.[3] For reference, the tallest basketball players to ever play in the NBA—Gheorghe Muresan and Manute Bol—were only seven feet, seven inches tall.[4] To read about the size of Goliath the giant for yourself, check out 1 Samuel 17:4.

they say, "But I'm too young!" when faced with tough decisions; God gave them the courage they needed to stand tall in the face of fear and intimidation.

You may have been in a situation where you felt pressured to join with other kids who were talking badly about someone. Or maybe you chose to hurt someone, either physically or emotionally, in another way. I think back to my earlier days, when the younger version of Evil Levi was running around with bullies, and I wish I would've made different choices. That said, I also know that every kid experiences peer pressure and makes mistakes—but it's never too late to turn things around.

If you feel like you lack courage, young warrior, ask God to fill your heart with bravery. Here's a prayer we can say together right now:

Dear God, give me the courage to make good decisions and to act bravely when the time comes. In Jesus' name, amen.

Eventually, when you choose it enough times, bravery will become automatic. It will become part of your being, like the way Superman just *is* a superhero. Acting with courage the first few times—and maybe even the first thousand times—won't be easy. Full disclosure: It might feel unbearable. But do it long enough and you will be only a little uncomfortable. Eventually you'll feel unstoppable. When you commit yourself to the process, you'll feel like David when he exclaimed, "With your help I can attack an army. With God's help I can jump over a wall" (Psalm 18:29 ICB).

A week after Papa Chuck's pep talk, Luca's soccer team divided into two groups for a scrimmage. Luca had kept his distance from the older guys for the last few days, hoping they would ignore him or forget about the incident with the cell phone—and for the most part, they had left him alone. But as Luca lined up and realized his side faced off against both Dylan and Finn, his breath caught.

"Think you can outrun us, loser?" Dylan yelled toward Luca as they jogged to their field positions.

Luca spotted Finn at the opposing goal, cracking his knuckles as if he had something to prove. These guys were older and taller than Luca, but soccer wasn't about size. It was about skill, and Luca had been practicing every single day.

As soon as Luca had possession of the ball, he trapped it under his foot. Then, in a blur of movement, he dribbled the ball cleanly past Dylan. Dylan spun around, shocked, as Luca danced past him and closed the gap between himself and the goal.

Luca pulled off a slick fake and an even better shot. Finn stumbled and lunged the wrong way as the ball sailed past him. It flew straight into the back of the net, and the other guys on Luca's team sprinted over with high fives.

Dylan and Finn both stood frozen, disbelief written on their faces. Luca walked past them without saying a word. There was no need to gloat; his skills were speaking for themselves.

Luca scored another goal during the scrimmage and managed three assists too. When his dad picked him up afterward, Luca filled him in on the plays he'd made that had contributed to his side winning. He was feeling strong and confident, having done his best on the field. Then his thoughts turned back to his teammates Dylan and Finn.

"Dad?" Luca said, catching his father's eyes in the rearview mirror. "Did Papa Chuck tell you he talked to me the other night?"

"He sure did, Chipper," Dad said. "He told me you did something brave, and I agree with him."

Luca slumped a little. "I didn't feel very brave," he admitted.

"Well, you were not only brave enough to stand up to those guys, but you were brave enough to talk to Papa Chuck about what happened. Those are two courageous moves right there." Dad flicked on his turn signal and switched lanes. "Plus, I'd say Papa Chuck knows a thing or two about bravery," Dad said. "He had a long military career, you know. And when I was about your age, he went overseas and supported combat operations in Desert Storm. He's even got a service medal to prove it."

Luca nodded, feeling proud of his grandad's legacy and thinking back over his encouraging words:

"Bravery is like a muscle," he'd said. *"The more you use it, the stronger it gets."*

GET READY FOR BATTLE

There is strength in numbers. You might be strong yourself, but with a friend—or two or three—your strength multiplies far beyond what you can do on your own. When it comes to doing hard things and having courage, you need *numbers*, little warrior. You need friends to stand with you in the battles you will face. Do you have those friends now? If not, think about who they could be, and pray for God's help to build your dynamic duo . . . or even a fantastic four!

STRATEGY 8

PLAN FOR LIFE'S RESPONSIBILITIES

After the debacle with her science project, Coral and her parents took a little time each Sunday afternoon to look over her homework schedule and make sure she was on track with her long-term assignments. For a little while, Coral felt more organized and more secure in her responsibilities, and her grades began to reflect the effort she was making.

But occasionally, something fell through the cracks.

One Wednesday after lunch, Coral walked back into class and slid into her seat.

"Okay, everyone," Mrs. Patel announced. "Clear your desks except for your pencils."

Coral was confused, but she did as she was told. Then, a moment later, Mrs. Patel placed what looked like a test in front of her.

What is this?! Coral scanned the classroom to see if anyone else looked surprised, but the other students seemed calm, cool, and collected. No one else appeared panicked at all.

"Eyes down, Coral," Mrs. Patel said.

Once again, Coral looked over the papers in front of her—two pages, front and back, stapled together in the top-left corner. This was no pop quiz; it was a full-on social studies test.

One she hadn't prepared for.

Coral's hand shook a little as she picked up her pencil and tried to make sense of the words in front of her. Social studies had always been a tough subject for Coral because of all the memorization it required. She usually enjoyed the lessons Mrs. Patel taught, but the tests still demanded Coral's attention and preparation. As she scanned the questions in front of her—a combination of multiple choice and short answer—her heart thumped harder in her chest.

She could answer some of these from memory, but many she could not.

For the next half hour, she racked her brain for any information that would help her with the questions. She made some educated guesses but also left a handful of spaces blank. By the time she handed her test to Mrs. Patel, Coral was so worked up she wondered whether she was going to melt into a puddle on the floor.

She turned toward her friend Millie, sitting to her left.

"Psst, Millie," she whispered. "Did you study for that test?"

"Yeah! It was so easy, huh? I took home that study sheet Mrs. Patel gave us and went over it with my mom last night."

"Uh-huh, yep, so easy," Coral lied. She turned back to face the front, trying to remember where she had put the study sheet from Mrs. Patel. It frustrated her even more when she realized she had no memory of it.

Coral spent the rest of the day in a funk, wondering where she'd gone wrong. When it was finally—*finally!*—time to leave that afternoon and she was packing up her backpack, she spotted a whole stack of papers lodged in the back of her assigned cubby.

Her eyes widened. Was *that* where the sheet had gone?

Hoping no one was looking, she reached into the cubby, took hold of

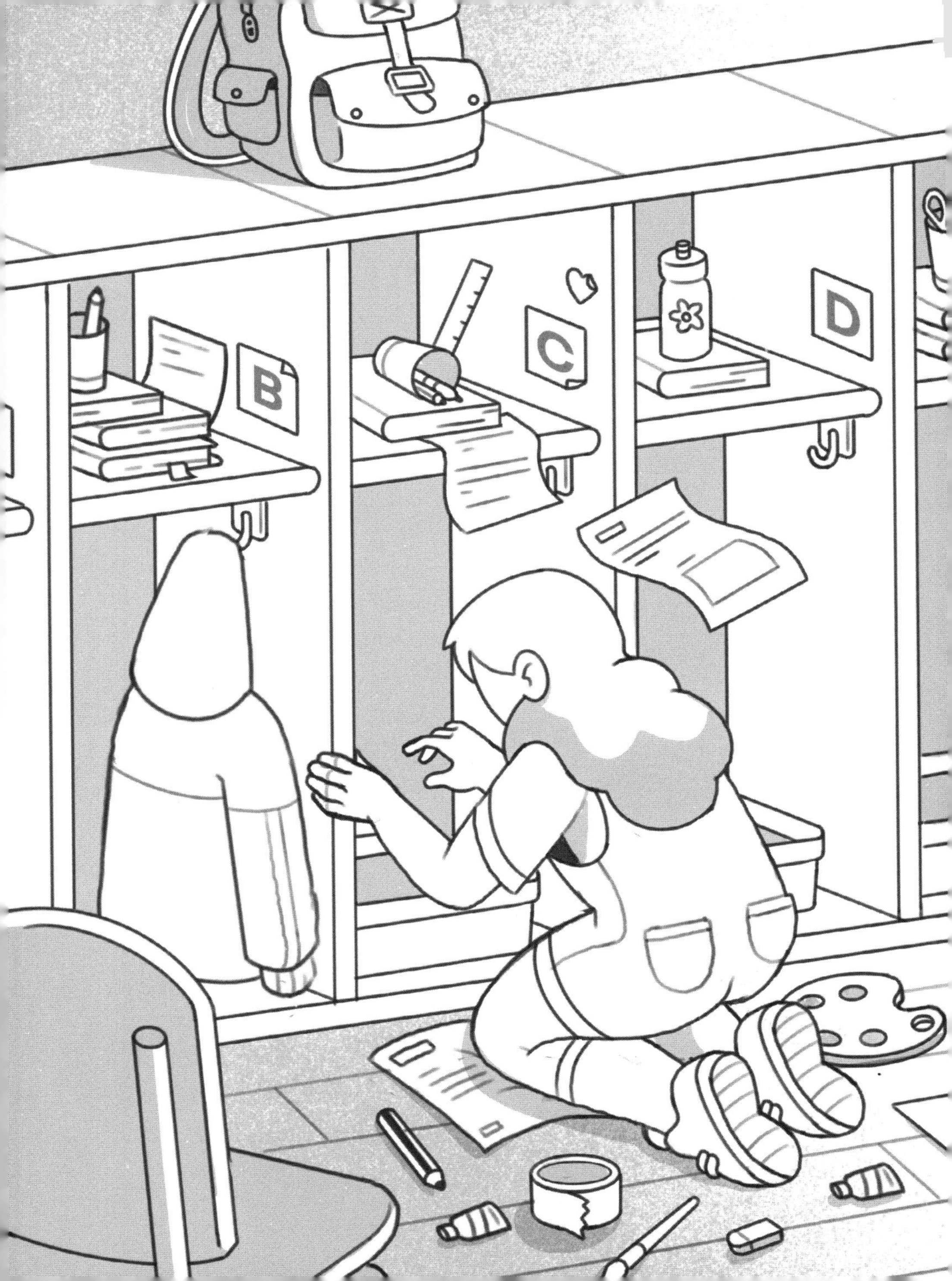
B
C
D

the papers, and shoved them into the bottom of her backpack. She would take everything out when she got home and give it all a better look.

All the way home, as Coral stared out the school bus window, her stomach continued to churn. She wished she could pretend that test had never happened, but her parents would find out about her grade eventually. *Is it better to come clean now or later?* she wondered. Either way, the situation stank. She'd made some progress organizing her responsibilities, but she clearly had more work to do.

As it turned out, Coral's mom figured it out pretty quickly. That afternoon, while Coral and Cami were playing outside in the last piles of leaves for the season, Mom stepped out the back door.

"Coral!" she hollered. "What on earth is this?"

Coral looked up. Mom was clutching a stack of papers in her hand.

"I . . . uh . . . uhhh—" Coral stammered. The stress of the day suddenly poured over her again, and she felt her cheeks getting hot.

"Please come inside and explain this to me," Mom said.

Cami giggled. "Uh-oh, sister's in trouble," she said, then plopped down on the cool autumn grass.

Coral trudged forward, shoulders slumped, and explained to Mom how she'd found the papers in her cubby that afternoon. As Mom listened, she shook her head.

"Well, Mrs. Patel just emailed me saying she hadn't received a permission slip for you to go to the corn maze next week," she said, laying the stack of papers on the kitchen counter. "So I decided to check your backpack and found this." She began looking through the sheets one by one.

Coral spotted the study sheet she'd been looking for among the pile. *Whoops*, she thought. *Too late now.*

"Why did these wind up in the back of your cubby in the first place?" Mom asked.

Coral shrugged. "I dunno . . . I guess I just wasn't thinking when I left them there."

Mom sighed, dropping an elbow on the counter and resting her forehead in her hand. "I know we've made some progress organizing your schoolwork, but Coral, this messiness and thoughtlessness is something I can't help you with. And I gotta tell you—I'm having enough trouble keeping my own life organized with my new job. Working, taking care of you, Cami, and Matteo, *and* doing my share of the housework is a lot." She closed her eyes and sighed again, deeper this time. "I think we need some better solutions here."

Since Coral was already in the deep end, she figured it was as good a time as any to tell her mom about the test she'd just flunked. Mom seemed so worn out that she barely flinched at the news.

"Okay, well, sounds like you gotta take the L on that one," she said.

"The L?"

"The loss," Mom said. "You can't undo it, but maybe you can do better next time." She rubbed her temples as if she suddenly had a headache. "Let me talk to your dad tonight about a plan. For now, please take this stack of papers and try to make sense of them. And find me that permission slip to sign while I finish with dinner."

Coral was grateful her mom wasn't angry, but her stress didn't seem to dissipate as she rifled through the wrinkled papers in front of her. *Why am I like this?* Coral thought. She knew her mom loved her but hated that she had disappointed her. Despite all the work she and her family had done, why was she still such a disorganized mess?

PRACTICING PREPAREDNESS

Do you relate to Coral's struggles with organization? My guess is you do because most people do (grown-ups included!). The older you get, the more responsibilities you tend to have on your plate—so it's no surprise that someone in your family might be trying to reorganize a closet, color-code a daily schedule, or keep a running list of items needed from the grocery store. With so much going on, it's easy to forget something important. And that's as true for adults as it is for someone your age.

This chapter isn't just about organization and tidiness; it's about having a mindset of preparedness. We've talked a lot about *practice* in this book—practicing good decision-making and bravery, for example—and now we will discuss practicing preparedness. What I mean by *preparedness* is the little steps you take each day to make sure you're ready for "game time" or "show time": the daily habits and choices that make it easier to perform your best when it matters most.

The real bulk of our lives is made of unglamorous, unspectacular, maybe even boring opportunities to make better choices that ultimately make our lives better. That's what I want to talk to you about in this chapter—not what happens on the court or the field of the stadium, where the cameras are recording and the crowds are cheering, but what you go through during the drive to the stadium, what happens in your head in the locker room, and how you feel at 4:00 A.M. when your alarm goes off and more than anything in the world you don't want to get up and practice. I want to talk about the game before the game.

If you look at someone who's crazy talented and doing something seemingly impossible—be it a figure skater, a freestyle rapper, or an ice sculptor—and you watch them perform for five minutes, remember that you are probably looking at a few thousand hours of work for every one of those eye-dazzling minutes. The work they do ahead of time gives them success when the cameras are rolling, the spectators are cheering, and their fans are handing them teddy bears and flowers.

So what about you? What do you want to do well, and how can you go about preparing for it?

WARRIOR CHALLENGE

Spend a few minutes thinking about one of your dreams or goals. It can be big ("I want to be an Olympian one day"), medium-size ("I want a speaking role in the school play"), or small ("I want to earn enough money for a new Switch game"). Write down your goal or dream. Then, brainstorm some ideas for all the ways you can prepare to meet that goal.

MY DREAM OR GOAL

_____

_____

STEPS I CAN TAKE TOWARD MY GOAL

1. _____
2. _____
3. _____
4. _____
5. _____

Everyone should have dreams and goals. They make life exciting, fun, and satisfying! But part of growing up is learning how to balance chasing our dreams with managing our responsibilities—the tasks, routines, and steps we must take every day to make life easier for ourselves and others. An important part of being a warrior is learning to be responsible. Cleaning up your own messes is a responsibility. Doing your homework is a responsibility. Brushing your teeth and doing chores at home are responsibilities. These tasks may not be the most thrilling, but if you don't do them, life can get pretty chaotic, messy, and confusing.

Here's the main difference between dreams and responsibilities though: You choose your dreams and goals, but you don't always choose your responsibilities. Most of us don't dream about cleaning our rooms, after all—but we *do* dream about writing a book, getting into a college, becoming a pilot, or learning to do a double-twisting double-tucked salto backward dismount like Simone Biles. (I dare you to say that five times fast!)

But here's how dreams and responsibilities are similar (and connected): They both demand work and preparation. And when we manage our responsibilities well, we will usually have more time and energy to devote to our passions and dreams.

You know how good it feels to finish your homework early so you can go practice your kickflips at the skate park? That's what I'm talking about.

Growing up is about learning to plan for life's responsibilities so we can also prepare for our wildest dreams. The bridge between all that practice and the performance is the pregame routine, young warrior.

Now let's talk about some practical ways you can get yourself ready for what's in front of you.

LET'S GET BATTLE-READY

Do you want to hear the good news or the bad news first, warrior?

Okay, let's get the bad news over with: Tackling life's responsibilities is something you'll face your entire life. Your parents have responsibilities, and your grandparents have them too. So do your teachers, coaches, counselors, and heroes. (Even Justin Bieber and Dwayne "The Rock" Johnson have responsibilities.)

But here's the good news: The more effort you put into managing your responsibilities now, the better you'll manage them as you get older. Like the other good habits we've discussed, your practice in this area will pay off big-time in the near future (today and tomorrow) as well as the far-off future (years from now).

So, without further ado, here are some tips for getting battle-ready.

1. Breathe Deeply

I know, we've already talked about breathing—but that's because it's a really important step toward tackling a problem, especially one that brings you stress!

Did you know that 20 percent of all oxygen you breathe goes straight to the brain? Your body's priority is to keep you alive, and it's always going to dedicate and divert the bulk of oxygen coming into critical life-saving functions.[1] So if you're breathing shallowly, the result is a loss of memory, a loss of focus, and a loss of power to overcome your moods. It also brings a heightened sense of anxiety.

Taking a deep breath is the easiest, quickest way to calm your heart rate. So try to remind yourself whenever you are feeling anxious that taking a series of long inhales and exhales can help you feel better in the moment. I've heard different numbers, but twelve seconds is a good one to shoot for, with a formula of 3–4–5: breathing in for three seconds, holding it for four, and then out for five seconds. Why don't you try it with me right now? Let's go:

Inhale: 1 . . . 2 . . . 3 . . .
Hold it: 1 . . . 2 . . . 3 . . . 4 . . .
Exhale: 1 . . . 2 . . . 3 . . . 4 . . . 5 . . .
I feel a little better. Don't you?

2. Get Organized

Now let's get down to the nitty-gritty. Some of you may be blessed with organized parents or guardians; others of you may not. (As I said, grown-ups can be disorganized too!) If you are struggling to keep your assignments and schedule in order, ask for help from a responsible adult. If your family needs help in this area, too, your teacher or school counselor may have resources for you as well.

Here are some ideas to try to get more organized today:

- Work with your family to create a **schedule** that includes your assignments, tests, extracurriculars, and church activities. Maybe you need a schedule of your own, or you can share a calendar with your family. This can be done on paper or digitally.

+ Gather your papers together and **organize** them in a way that makes sense to you (try using a binder, planner, folders, etc.). Or, if it's easier and you have access to the technology needed to make it happen, try digitizing everything instead. Ask your parents or a trusted adult for help finding a homework or calendar app that might work for you.

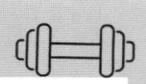

+ If you have a locker, a desk, or a cubby at school, make sure to **clean** it out regularly. Likewise, if you have a spot at home where many of your papers and junk tend to land, make a plan to clean it out at least once a week.

TACTICAL TRAINING

Clutter is a big enemy of organization. You get everything sorted, organized, put away, and then—boom: Your teacher hands you *another* stack of papers. Here's a tip: Add a "Declutter Day" to your weekly schedule. Set a timer for fifteen minutes, and use that time to empty your backpack, your cubby, your locker—wherever you store your stuff—and get rid of everything you don't need. Recycle what you can. Trash the rest. You can do it, warrior! Staying on top of clutter will make your job of staying organized *way* more manageable!

3. Manage Your Time

This is where your calendar and schedule come in handy. Take a look at what you have to get done and estimate how much time your responsibilities will take. This is a step an adult could help you with because adults (usually!) have a better sense of time.

Time management is one of those life skills that just takes practice. If you feel like you never have enough time to study or finish your schoolwork, it may be time to seek help from a parent or trusted adult. Even a warrior needs help now and then. Sometimes, when we have too much to do, we have to decide what matters most and let go of less important activities. These are conversations that need to be had honestly with the people who take care of you.

Some schools have resources for students who struggle with time management. If you feel stressed because you never seem to be on time for anything, ask a teacher or counselor to see what resources are available at your school. Managing your time well today sets you up for success tomorrow, and teachers love nothing more than helping you prepare for future wins.

4. Strike a Pose

Trying to get organized and manage your time can be crazy hard. And sometimes, when we fall short or realize our methods aren't yet working (think about Coral and her social studies test!), we can wind up feeling overwhelmed, anxious, and stressed all over again.

Here's a little tip I learned from a woman named Amy Cuddy, who gave a viral talk called "Your Body Language May Shape Who You Are." (Ask a parent to look it up on YouTube!)[2] You may have noticed that when you are worried or stressed, you want to curl up into a little ball. Your shoulders slump, you hunch over, you may even tuck your chin. But that posture cascades into more nervousness because of the release of cortisol (stress) into your system. And the last thing we need when we are stressed is *more stress*!

What Amy Cuddy discovered is that putting your hands on your hips like Wonder Woman or up in the air (picture someone who just scored a touchdown or aced a test) can dramatically change how you feel. When you do this, your body's hormones change in as little as 120 seconds. It's as if you're saying to your body, "Get outta here, stress! I don't need you right now! I have important things to do!"

I was completely shocked when I initially watched this video, but the first thing I thought of was the book of Psalms. It is full of commands to praise God with raised hands and heads held high. You won't find a psalm that tells you to tuck yourself into a ball and sing to God meekly with your hands in your pockets. It's all about shouting with a voice of triumph and raising arms to the Lord.

Next time you find yourself feeling defeated, check your posture. Are you standing tall like a warrior? If you're slumped over, try posing as if you're David preparing to fire his slingshot. Stay in that pose for a couple of minutes and remind yourself that even if you are struggling to manage your feelings, thoughts, and responsibilities, you've got a powerful God who's on your side and *wants* to see you win.

And if you think about it, that's the best kind of victory of all.

The next day at school, Mrs. Patel handed back Coral's test. It wasn't a good grade, but it also wasn't the worst Coral had ever seen. She remembered what her mother had said about "taking the L"—how some mistakes can't be undone and shouldn't be sources of constant stress. So she sighed and slid the paper into her binder, hoping to put the past behind her while resolving to study, prepare, and do better next time.

Back at home that evening, Mom called Coral into the kitchen as she stirred a pot of chili on the stovetop.

"So I'm not sure how you'll feel about this," Mom said, "but I've made an appointment for you and me to see the school counselor, Mr. Woods."

Coral made a face. "The counselor? For what?"

"Well, as it turns out, he's got some resources for students who need a little help in the time management and organization department," she responded. "He said he can help us with some routines and habits that may work better for you."

The thought of seeing a counselor made Coral feel self-conscious. "But I don't want special help, Mom," she confessed. "That makes me feel . . ."

Mom stepped across the kitchen and placed a hand gently on Coral's cheek. "Hey, this is nothing to be stressed about. We're trying to help you feel *less* stressed. Look me in the eye for a second."

Coral looked up at her mom.

"Repeat after me," she said. "Brave people ask for help."

"Brave people ask for help," Coral repeated.

"Now, stand up straight and say, 'I've got this.'"

Coral squared up her posture and grinned. "I've got this," she said.

Coral closed her eyes as her mother said a short prayer over her, thanking God for giving them the help they needed and asking Him for strength and courage. As her mother ended the prayer, Coral took a deep, calming breath. It was going to be okay, she knew. She had parents who loved her, teachers who wanted to help her, and a God who wanted the best for her.

"Now, scoot back to that study table, kiddo!" Mom said, playfully pinching Coral's ear.

And Coral did exactly that. She cracked open her textbook, turned to the right page, and prepared herself for tomorrow's work.

GET READY FOR BATTLE

Do you prefer to think of yourself as an athlete preparing for a game? Or a warrior preparing for battle? Either way works as you consider how to slay your own list of goals, tasks, and responsibilities. And what every great hero (or athlete) needs to perform their best is a motto. Before I do hard things, I love to remind myself that "I can do all things through Christ because he gives me strength" (Philippians 4:13 ICB) and that I am as "bold as a lion" (Proverbs 28:1 NIV). Coral practiced saying "Brave people ask for help" and "I've got this." Choose your own battle-ready catchphrase today. And write it down here:

_____

STRATEGY 9

GIVE YOUR WORRIES TO GOD

By the middle of November, Luca was wrapping up his final week of soccer. He had one more game before Thanksgiving, and the trees had given up most of their colorful leaves. Though Luca hated for the soccer season to end, he was already looking forward to spending the holidays with his big, loud extended family, who would travel from all over the country to celebrate together at his home.

Like most kids this time of year, he was also ready for a break from school.

At his last game, he scored a goal in the final minutes and waved to his parents and sister, Anna, in the stands. Sometimes he felt embarrassed that they cheered so loudly for him, but deep down, he enjoyed having fans—even if they *were* just his family.

After the game, they drove to a burger place that served Luca's favorite crinkle fries. Almost starving, Luca could barely hold himself back from swallowing his cheeseburger in one bite. As he was halfway through his triple chocolate milkshake, he heard his dad clear his throat.

"So, kids, I've got something I need to tell you," he began. Luca looked up from his near-empty plate and noticed that his dad's face looked a little somber. He and Anna locked eyes across the table, and Luca was suddenly filled with concern.

"I don't want you to worry," Dad continued, "because it's all going to be fine. I promise. But since you're both old enough to understand now . . ." Dad hesitated, as if the words were hard for him to say. "Well, I lost my job yesterday."

Luca was speechless. He looked up at his dad, then his mom, who gave a small reassuring smile, then sipped her Diet Coke. "It's just one of those things," she said. "He'll find another job. And if he doesn't, I will." She turned her head and winked at Dad.

Anna seemed a bit teary at the news, but Dad quickly put an arm around her. "Oh, honey, please don't be upset. Mom's right, Annabelle. I'm already looking for another job. And we've got savings to carry us over until then." Anna looked up at him, her doe eyes still filling, and Dad kissed the top of her head. "Really. It's gonna be fine."

"We aren't trying to upset you kids," Mom said. "But we decided you had a right to hear about it from us. And since you're old enough to understand the situation, we may need your help cutting some costs here and there. Nothing big. But we have to be extra wise about how we spend our money."

Luca didn't quite know what to say, having never been in this position before. Should he be anxious? Scared? He believed his parents, and he didn't have a reason to doubt them when they told them not to worry. But he couldn't help but notice that his dad's face seemed ashen, and his eyes a little sad.

On the way home, Luca's thoughts spun as they often did. But this time, he imagined worst-case scenarios. What if Dad *never* got a job again? What if they couldn't pay their bills? Would they have to give up Christmas presents? Or move in with Nana and Papa Chuck?

The next afternoon, his grandparents stopped by the house on their way home from church. The day had been cold and rainy, so Luca had blown a lot of his allotted weekly screen time playing *Minecraft* on the iPad.

Papa Chuck found Luca in his room. As he stepped inside, he knocked on the doorframe. Luca looked up from the iPad and laughed when he saw his grandad wearing a loud sweater with a wolf howling at the moon embroidered on it.

Papa Chuck held out his arms to show off his outfit. "Whaddya think of my fire sweater, Chipper? Do I pass the fit check? Is it a vibe?"

Luca laughed so quickly he snorted and made a feigned disgusted face. "Oh, it's definitely something . . ."

Papa Chuck laughed. "I read an article about youngsters' new slang and thought I would try some out."

"Nice, Papa."

His grandpa sat down near Luca on the floor. They both looked at Luca's *Minecraft* build before talking about how he'd scored a goal in yesterday's game.

"I'm sorry I couldn't be there," Papa Chuck said. "But I heard about your great play. And I heard your dad told you the news about his job."

Luca nodded and looked down at his lap. Though he'd tried hard not to worry, his imagination was not helping him. "Is Dad gonna be okay?" he asked.

"Yes, he will," said Papa Chuck. "That's what I wanted to tell you. He'll be fine, and so will you, Anna, and your mom. We'll help you in whatever way is needed. And I'm praying for you too. In fact, we said a special prayer for your family today in my small group at church."

Luca didn't really understand what prayer was all about. He knew his grandparents went to church every Sunday because they talked about it and often talked about God. From what Luca could tell, praying was a bit like having a conversation with God—but since he'd never tried it, he wasn't sure how it was supposed to go.

Even more, he wasn't totally sure who or what God was.

"I hope you'll trust me when I say you don't need to worry," Papa Chuck continued. "I know you tend to get anxious about some things, Chipper, but that's a tendency you got from me." He nudged his shoulder and winked. "Nana and I will always do what we can to help, and God is going to take care of your family too."

THE ONE AND ONLY INCREDIBLE GOD

So far in this book, we've covered the importance of managing our feelings, words, and actions in order to grow and thrive. Thinking positively is important, as is watching how you speak and practicing good habits. But if that is all you walk away with, then this book would not be complete. While you and I can do so much to help ourselves, we can't do it all on our own.

We need God's help for everything. He loves us, wants the best for us, and makes it all possible.

Have you heard the expression "never bring a horse to a tank fight"? Think about it for a minute. Horses are great and all, but a battle tank is *huge*. Its whole deal is to run over things, hit targets, and sustain heavy fire from opponents—so a horse really can't compete. Trying to win a tank battle with a horse would be like trying to dig a ditch with a spoon rather than a shovel. Sometimes you just need the right equipment to get the job done!

As we fight life's battles, having better weapons in our arsenal will improve our likelihood of success. Being more in control of our emotions and habits will help us get through each day with fewer battle scars. But when the war rages and even our most well-practiced resources aren't enough, we have one weapon that is more powerful than all others: The kind of wisdom and strength that comes only from God and His Word. A warrior like you can't get any finer weapon than the Word of God!

God is incredible. Picture your favorite superhero and multiply their power by infinity. Or imagine God as the best game designer ever, except instead of video games, He's designed . . . well, everything

THINK LIKE A WARRIOR

If you could go back in time twenty-five years, the iPhone wouldn't exist. And if you could go back one hundred years, you wouldn't find microwaves, Scotch tape, or even sliced bread! But that doesn't mean everything we use today is new to our century.

For example, have you ever thought about how long the Bible—the Word of God—has been around? The books of the Bible were all written at different times by different people, but they were all inspired by God Himself. The oldest book of the Bible may have been written as long as *three thousand years ago*.[1] How cool is it to know that the most important book ever written has been changing the world for generations and generations?

around you. God imagined the whole universe, spoke it into being, and now watches over it all the time from everywhere. God is so amazing that He's actually impossible to comprehend. The very fact that He's too big, too awesome, too artful, too wise, and too strong for us to even imagine is what makes him God and us His beloved creations.

Let's pause here to give you the chance to write down some thoughts on God. Maybe you've thought a lot about the God who made you, or maybe you haven't thought too much about Him at all. Either way, who do you think God is, and what do you think He is like?

God is . . .

_____

_____

_____

God is like . . .

_____

_____

_____

God can . . .

_____

_____

_____

God loves . . .

_____

_____

_____

No matter what you wrote down, I guarantee God is even more humongous, more next-level, more crazy good than that. As a warrior, you will want to enlist God's help in all your battles. He's too *everything* for our minds to even comprehend.

So can you imagine having a better source of strength for life's battles? I sure can't.

WHAT WE DO VS. WHAT GOD DOES

When Jesus was living on earth, He worked all kinds of miracles that proved to people around Him that He is the Son of God. He walked on water, He healed the sick and disabled, and He made food appear out of nowhere. But perhaps most miraculous of all is His ability to bring the dead back to life.

One person He brought back to life was a little girl. The Bible tells us she was twelve years old, and her dad, Jairus, was a synagogue ruler. (A *synagogue* is where Jewish people worshiped God.) Jairus came to find Jesus, asking Him to cure his daughter before she died. But while Jairus and Jesus were making their way to the girl's home, some men who worked for Jairus found him and said, "Your daughter is dead. There is now no need to bother the teacher" (Mark 5:35 ICB).

No parent can imagine hearing worse words than these. We don't know for sure, but we can imagine Jairus weeping at this devastating news about his beloved child.

But here's what the Bible says happened next:

Jesus paid no attention to what the men said. He said to the synagogue ruler, "Don't be afraid; only believe." Jesus let only Peter, James, and John the brother of James go with him to Jairus's house. They came to the house of the synagogue ruler, and Jesus found many people there crying loudly. There was much confusion. Jesus entered the house and said to the people, "Why are you crying and making so much noise? This child is not dead. She is only asleep." But they only laughed at Jesus. He told all the people to leave. Then he went into the room where the child was. He took the child's father and mother and his three followers into the room with him. Then he took hold of the girl's hand and said to her, "Talitha, koum!" (This means, "Little girl,

I tell you to stand up!") The girl stood right up and began walking. (Mark 5:36–42 ICB)

Can you imagine how shocked and amazed everyone must have been? Jesus had done the unthinkable and defied the laws of nature. The household's tears of sorrow suddenly became tears of joy—all because of the miraculous healing power of God's one and only Son.

The story of the healed little girl ends with "Jesus [giving] the father and mother strict orders not to tell people about this. Then he told them to give the girl some food" (v. 43 ICB). We don't know why Jesus asked them not to tell anyone what had happened, but we do know why He told the parents to feed their daughter. Humans need food to survive—and now that Jairus's daughter was alive and well again, she was probably hungry and needed a snack!

This little girl could not have brought herself back to life. Aside from Jesus, no one in history has been able to do that—never before and never since. Without God, we are similarly hopeless, lost, and completely unable to change our state. So why, then, did Jesus raise her from the dead but tell her parents to feed her?

Because God won't do for you what you can do for you. He does the super things but expects us to do the natural things.

I share this story to point out that God can do more than we can even imagine. At the same time, He has given us some really handy tools—and it is our responsibility to make the best use of them. We can do our part, but God will always do the bigger part. And with a little faith and God's help and blessing, we can do immeasurably more than we ever could on our own.

> **WARRIOR CHALLENGE**
>
> Dream big. You've probably heard that phrase before, but what about "pray big"? Whatever obstacle you or your family is up against, God is bigger. So pray big—a warrior-sized prayer. Ask God to work in you in a big way, to make a big change, or to show you the bigger picture when it comes to your fears. He may not answer the way you want or in the time frame you want, but He *is* listening, and He's not intimidated by your big prayers!

WHEN YOU AREN'T IN CONTROL

Have you ever heard of someone being referred to as a *control freak*? I'll tell you this much: It's not usually a compliment. To be a control freak is to be obsessed with making sure everything happens according to your wishes and preferences. You want to be in charge of everything; you want to be the boss. And a control freak usually flies off the handle (a.k.a. flips out) when something doesn't go the way they want it to.

As we've discussed, kids aren't in charge of everything in their lives because adults are often making decisions for them. For example, if it were up to you, a school day might just be several hours of snacks and recess, followed by a field trip to Six Flags or Disney World. (That'd be a great school day, by the way.)

But as you get older, you are given more responsibilities, which means more decisions and control too. Learning how to make good choices now is good practice for making more and more good choices in the future.

I've got a little secret, though—a message from adulthood that you may not want to hear. Are you ready?

Grown-ups aren't always in control either.

"Hold up, what?" you may be saying. "How is that possible?"

Let me give you an example of what I mean.

Pretend I'm an adult. (I am, by the way.) I've got an appointment to see the dentist at 3:00 p.m., and I know it will take thirty minutes to get there. Just to be safe, in case there is some traffic, I leave my house forty-five minutes before the appointment. But as I'm pulling out of the driveway—

Screech! Crunch! Clatter!

Another driver was speeding down the hill and hit my car. Does it seem like I'll be making it to my appointment on time?

The big secret is that no matter how much we plan or practice, sometimes life throws you curveballs. Accidents happen. People get sick. Parents lose jobs. We drop the beautiful iced birthday cake we just bought when we slip on a banana peel in the parking lot. (Or does that just happen in cartoons?)

The list could go on and on. My point is this: Life is full of the unexpected. No matter how organized, skilled, or control-freaky you are, you can expect to be surprised by something almost every day of your life.

Some of us are pretty good at dealing with life's blows. *Resilient* is a word that describes people who are good at adapting to change, and ultimately, that's a good quality to foster in oneself. But if you're anything like me, you have a different nature. Rather than adapting quickly, you worry. You stress out. Even when something bad hasn't happened yet, you expect that it will and spend a lot of energy imagining those potential scenarios.

What if something bad happens to someone I love?
What if the kids at school make fun of me?
What if this class is too hard for me?
What if my parents get divorced?

Fearing the unknown is normal. And these are all very real, legitimate concerns because they are outside of our control. You already know by now that sometimes bad things just happen; and even if they *haven't* happened, some of us mentally prepare ourselves for the possibility that they will.

But it is possible to give too much time and energy to these fearful thoughts. That's when a small worry turns into a big-time fear or even full-blown anxiety.

Warrior, I want to remind you that God's got this. When the world around you feels weird or off-kilter, God is there. When you're facing an unpredictable situation that is causing you stress, God is there. No matter what, God is there—and He has the supernatural power you need to conquer your fear and worry. He's the strongest weapon in your arsenal, if only you will call on Him to help.

Next time you are feeling unsure, call on God. Next time you are feeling nervous or afraid, call on God. Next time your worries are getting the best of you, call on God. Ask Him for comfort, strength, and peace. Remember King David? The boy who fought the giant and then became ruler of Israel? Here's what he wrote about God's ability to empower our daily battles:

> The ways of God are without fault.
>> The Lord's words are pure.
>> He is a shield to those who trust him.
>> Who is God? Only the Lord.
>> Who is the Rock? Only our God.
>> God is my protection.
>> He makes my way free from fault.
>> He makes me like a deer, which does not stumble.
>> He helps me stand on the steep mountains.
>> He trains my hands for battle.
>> So my arms can bend a bronze bow.
>> You protect me with your saving shield.
>> You support me with your right hand.
>> You have stooped to make me great.
>> You give me a wide path on which to walk.
>> My feet have not slipped. (Psalm 18:30–36 ICB)

Don't worry, warrior. With God on your side, you can face any battle. Let's practice a simple prayer you can use anytime you feel anxious or afraid:

> *Dear God, with your help, all things are possible. Today I am feeling _____ because _____. Please give me courage and strength as I face this battle. In Jesus' name, amen.*

Thanksgiving was fun as usual for Luca, as his cousins and aunts and uncles all descended upon their house for Turkey Day. Even his other grandparents, Nonna and Nonno, flew down from New York, and his Nonna taught him how to make her famous pignoli cookies. The house was filled with laughter and all kinds of delicious smells. But Luca couldn't help but notice that his dad still looked a little down.

Weeks passed, and his dad still hadn't found a new job. His parents tried their best not to act worried in front of him or Anna, but Luca heard them talking in hushed whispers about money and cutting back and how they were going to afford Christmas gifts. At the end of each day, Luca climbed into bed feeling helpless. Each time he lodged himself under the covers with his comic book and flashlight, he thought, *Superman could fix this. If only he were real . . .*

One Saturday night in December, his dad announced that they'd be attending church the next morning with Papa Chuck and Nana.

Luca tilted his head. "What'll it be like?" he asked.

"Well, there will be singing, and someone will teach a lesson. And if we like going to the service, maybe soon you and Anna will go to a class with other kids your age," he said.

"And Nana and Papa Chuck will go with us?" Anna asked excitedly. Luca found it funny that Anna was always excited about new things, regardless of whether she had a frame of reference for them.

"Yes," Dad said, laughing. "And maybe we'll have lunch together afterward."

The next morning after breakfast, everyone piled into the minivan and drove the short distance to the church building. On the far side of the parking lot they found Nana and Papa Chuck, who were climbing out of their own car. Papa Chuck was sporting another goofy outfit today—this time, a fluorescent shirt with a rubber-duckie necktie.

"Heyyy, Chipper!" Papa Chuck roared. "And hello to my little darling Annabelle."

Once inside the building, Luca felt a bit awkward because he wasn't sure what to do in the unfamiliar place. He followed his grandad's lead and took a seat in a cushiony chair. Glancing around, he spotted a girl with long black hair sitting a few feet away between two adults, a smaller girl, and a boy who might've been her teenage brother. She looked up and caught him staring, then gave a slight wave. He didn't know her name, but he'd seen her at school. So he waved a greeting back, and she smiled.

Church was not like he'd expected. He'd enjoyed the songs (though he didn't know any of them), and he had done his best to pay attention to the speaker. But the part he appreciated most was when the person with the microphone had led them in a prayer. When the man said, "Let's pray," Luca noticed Papa Chuck closing his eyes and bowing his head, so he did the same.

"Thank You, God, for loving us," said the speaker. "We know You can do all things, and we cast our cares on You."

Luca wasn't sure what "cast your cares" meant exactly, but he guessed it meant letting God know about your problems.

"We can do all things through Christ, who strengthens us," the man continued. "Give us the courage to do right and make our paths straight."

Luca wasn't quite following, so he let his mind wander. As he sat with

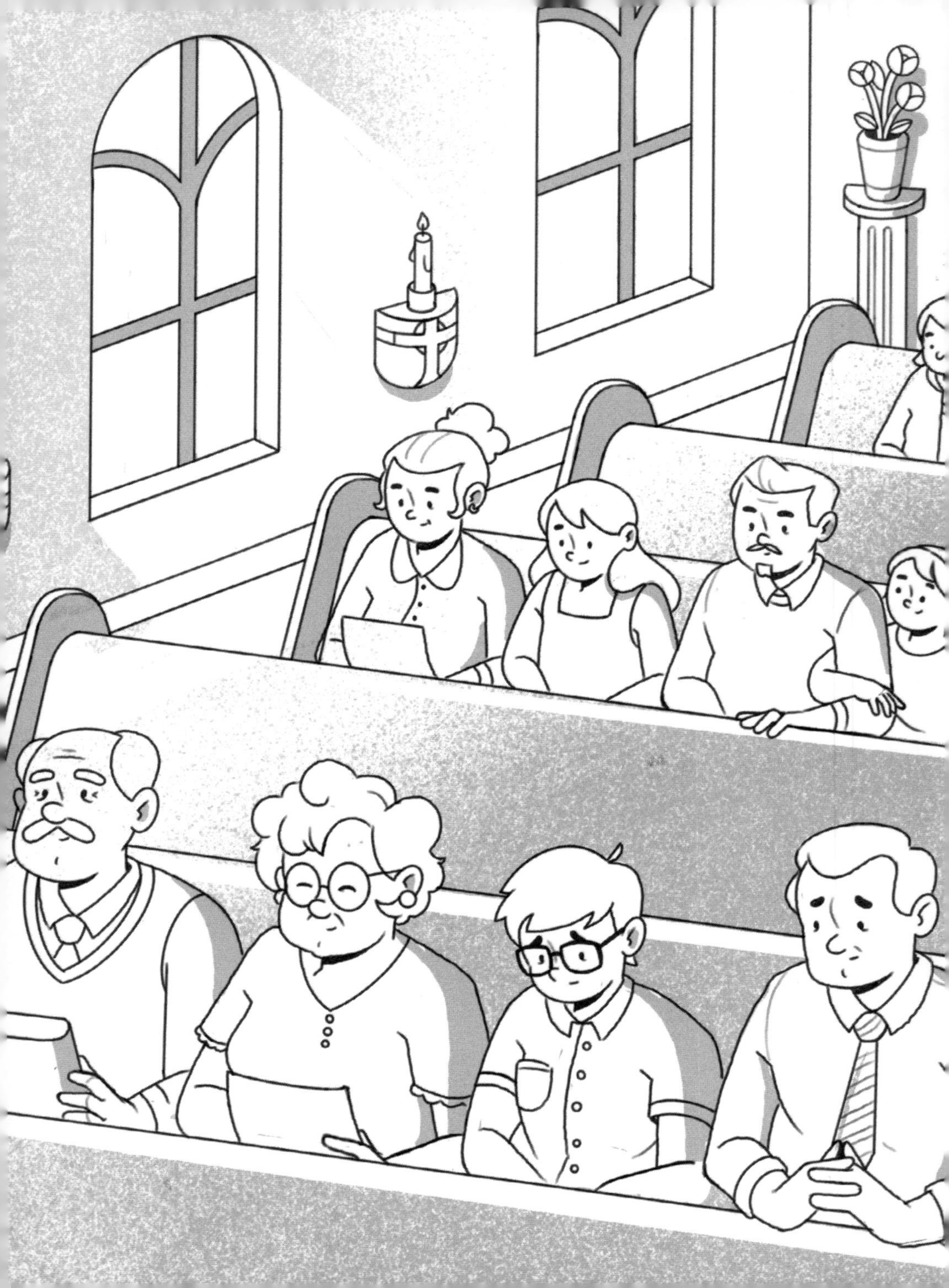

his eyes closed, he wondered about who God might be. If God had made the whole world and if God was in control of everything, could God take care of Luca and his family?

Without really knowing it, Luca said his first prayer.

God, please help my dad.

Nothing too exciting happened as Luca's heart lifted up this prayer. No lights went out, no earthquakes rumbled, and no stars fell from the sky. But Luca did feel a gentle sense of peace, almost like a soft breeze inside his heart.

Did You hear me, God? Are You there? Are You listening? Luca wondered.

And though Luca didn't know it for sure yet, God certainly was.

GET READY FOR BATTLE

What worry is on your heart today? Are you experiencing a family crisis like Luca or dealing with something more personal—maybe a falling out with your best friend or an upcoming recital that you're nervous about or a general feeling of anxiety that you can't explain? Whatever it is, young warrior, today is the day to give it to God. Prayer is one of the strongest weapons in a warrior's arsenal. Your prayer can be simple like Luca's or long like King David's. The important thing is to be honest, sharing all your thoughts, fears, and questions with your incredible God.

STRATEGY 10

TRUST GOD IN HARD TIMES

Have you ever had the wind knocked out of you?

For me, it always happened at recess, and it always involved falling—off a slide, off the swings, off a fence. I guess I just fell a lot as a kid. Seconds seemed like hours as I'd try to get my lungs to expand. I was sure I was going to die. This would continue for what seemed like an eternity, until all of a sudden everything would be okay—and then I'd immediately go back to playing, like nothing happened.

What I didn't know then was that there is more than one way to get the wind knocked out of you.

As I grew up, I dealt with harder things than falling. I had painful experiences and endured some losses so big I'll think about them every day for the rest of my life. *This is more than I can bear* has crossed my mind more times than I can count. Maybe you've already dealt with some really big things in your life—and if so, you know what I mean and how I felt. And if you haven't, well, you probably will one day. I don't say that to frighten or worry you; I want only to remind you that part of being human is learning to endure hard things.

That's why it is so important that you don't try to fight these battles in your own strength or by relying on your own lung power. When your breath is taken away, you need to rely on God for a second wind. The first wind is your natural air given to you at creation, when God breathed into the dust He formed us out of. The second wind is the power given to us after Jesus died and came back to life.

After Sunday morning church was over, Coral's family went to eat lunch at one of her older brother Matteo's favorite restaurants. They had placed their orders and were snacking on chips and salsa when Mom let everyone know that her sister, Serena, would be coming to stay with them for a while.

"Is she coming early for the holidays?" Coral asked. "Christmas is more than two weeks away."

Mom paused a moment, then sipped her ice water. "Well, yes, she will be here for Christmas," she said. "But that's not the whole reason she's coming."

"Why then?" asked Matteo.

Mom looked at Dad, as if unsure of what words to use. "Tía Serena just needs a place to stay for a while," she said. "And I told her she could stay with us."

"Why not at her house?" Cami asked. None of this was making much sense, especially to the littlest sibling.

"What about Tío Marco?" Coral asked. "Is he coming too?"

Mom shook her head. "No, he isn't," she said, then let out a long sigh. "The main reason she's coming is because she and Marco are talking about getting a divorce. So your aunt's just going to live with us while they make that decision."

"What'd he do?" Matteo said around a mouthful of chips.

"This is a private matter between them," Mom responded somewhat sternly. "So we aren't going to ask questions like that. Our job is to give her a place to feel at home."

Coral felt sadness swelling in her heart at the thought of her aunt and uncle splitting up. She had missed Marco and Serena so much since they'd moved from Texas, and now Coral wondered when she'd get to see her uncle again. At the same time, she understood these were adult problems. Adults were good at fixing things, so maybe her aunt and uncle would get back together. Surely, they would.

After lunch, Mom asked Coral and Matteo to help her tidy up the guest room for Tía Serena. "I'm not sure how long she'll stay with us," Mom said, "so let's make it as comfortable as possible for her."

They changed the sheets, dusted the nightstands, and fluffed the pillows to decorate the bed. Then, once the room was clean and comfortable, Coral enlisted Cami's help to hand-decorate a sign for the door that read, "Welcome to Tía Serena's Room."

Tía Serena pulled into the driveway just after dinner. Mom went outside alone to greet her, and Coral could see her mother giving Serena a big, long hug. Before she came inside, Serena wiped both eyes with the backs of her hands. But Coral could tell she had been crying.

Tía Serena gave big hugs to all the kids as Dad brought her bags in from the car. When she saw the sign Coral and Cami had made for her room, she looked ready to cry again.

"You girls are so sweet," she said, squeezing them both on the shoulders. "I've missed you so much, and I love you so."

"We love you too, Tía Serena," Coral said.

That night, after everyone's teeth were brushed and backpacks were all packed up for the next day, Mom sneaked into Coral's room and crouched down on the floor by her bed. The only light in the room came from Coral's rainbow unicorn lamp, which cast a warm glow across the bed.

"Thank you for helping me get ready for Tía Serena today," Mom said to Coral. "She's going through a hard time, but you made her feel welcome."

Coral shrugged. "I don't mind," she said. "I love Tía Serena."

Mom nodded. "Me too. Can we say a special prayer for her?"

Coral sat up in bed and bowed her head, and Mom took Coral's hand in her own. "Dear God," she began, "thank You for this lovely day. Thank You for Coral and her brother and sister. And thank You for bringing Tía Serena here safely." Mom paused, and her breath hitched slightly. Coral wondered whether her mom was trying not to cry.

"God, Tía Serena needs our love and care. Thank You for caring for her, and help us to be kind and gentle with her during this hard time. Please heal her heart, and Marco's too. Thank You for always giving us what we need. In Your Son's name we pray, amen."

Coral repeated her "amen," then looked up at her mom.

"Is Tía Serena really sad?" she asked, already knowing the answer.

"Yes, honey, she is," Mom said. "So we need to be extra kind and patient with her. But even though she's sad, I know she will be okay because we are looking out for her. And more importantly, God is too."

EVERY FAMILY HAS PROBLEMS

No family is just like the next, so your parents, grandparents, or guardians are different from the ones your best friends have. And that's okay! But here's something that's 100 percent true about all families and adults:

They have problems.

Some grown-up problems are small—traffic on the way to work, a headache, or lost car keys. But some are big—like a divorce, a loved one who passed away, a demanding job, or a financial concern that is probably too complicated (and too boring!) to fully explain. Parents may try to deal with their problems privately, while others deal with their problems more openly in front of their kids. Some parents show big feelings and emotions, while others tend to be more discreet. (That means they don't show their feelings as much.) But even if you have adults in your life who try not to worry you with the things they're dealing with, I can promise you this much: They *do* have problems to solve and painful experiences to endure. That's just part of being alive!

But here's the bottom line: Problems are easier to manage

> **THINK LIKE A WARRIOR**
>
> A fighter jet typically has two seats: one for the pilot and one for the other guy (known as the weapon systems operator). If you're the guy in the back seat, you're totally dependent on your pilot to keep you out of harm's way and to take you to the right spot when it's time to use your weapons. Consider this: Your battles as a warrior are more easily won when God is the pilot of your jet. While it can be hard to let someone else take the lead, especially when the battle rages and lives are at stake, who better to pilot you than God? He is all-knowing and all-powerful. No one can help a warrior like you navigate the hard times better than Him.

when God is on your side. That is just as true for someone your age as it is for your parents, teachers, coaches, grandparents, and the grouchy old man who lives down the street and is constantly yelling at you to *get off his lawn!*

God's got the power; you just need to ask for it. He is a good Father. He won't give you a tarantula if you ask for a Fruit Roll-Up. And He will give you strength and courage if you ask Him to.

Try it. And when you get the wind knocked out of you, ask for a second wind, and a third, and a fourth. If you're knocked down seven times, He'll give you an eighth wind too.

GOD KEEPS HIS PROMISES

Did you know the word *promise* shows up in the Bible hundreds of times? Most of the time, the word references a promise God made—and kept. Because God is perfect and knows everything, it would be against His nature to make a promise He couldn't keep. When He says He will do something, He does it. You can always count on Him.

In Jesus' Sermon on the Mount—one of the most important lessons He ever shared—He said this about God, His Father:

> I tell you, don't worry about the food you need to live. Don't worry about the clothes you need for your body. Life is more important than food. And the body is more important than clothes. Look at the birds. They don't plant or harvest. They don't save food in houses or barns. But God takes care of them. And you are worth much more

than birds. None of you can add any time to your life by worrying about it. If you cannot do even the little things, then why worry about the big things? Look at the wild flowers. See how they grow. They don't work or make clothes for themselves. But I tell you that even Solomon, the great and rich king, was not dressed as beautifully as one of these flowers. . . . So you know how much more God will clothe you. Don't have so little faith! Don't always think about what you will eat or what you will drink. Don't worry about it. All the people in the world are trying to get those things. Your Father knows that you need them. The thing you should seek is God's kingdom. Then all the other things you need will be given to you. (Luke 12:22–31 ICB)

Do you see what Jesus is promising? God cares for the birds and the flowers, but He cares for you way, *way* more. He made you, and He loves you, and He doesn't want you to spend your

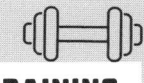

TACTICAL TRAINING

Something we've been learning about in this book is prayer. Coral and Luca are both learning how to turn to God when they are feeling anxious or afraid. God loves to hear from you, so it's never a bad idea to speak to Him with your words or in your thoughts.

If you're not in the habit of praying much, consider making yourself some reminders. Write a couple of short prayers or prompts on Post-it notes and stick them on your bathroom mirror or on your bedside table. The reminders can be short and simple, such as "Thank God for a blessing" or "Ask God for help with something." Giving yourself gentle nudges like this may turn you into a full-on praying warrior one day.

life feeling worried, anxious, or afraid. God cares for His children, and that means *you*. God thinks about you every second of every minute of every day—and I hope it brings comfort and peace to your mind to know that God can manage any worry, fear, or concern that may be troubling your heart.

All you have to do is ask for His help, young warrior.

As Christmastime neared, Coral's family did their best to celebrate with cheer. They watched Christmas movies, baked and decorated cookies, and drove around town to see the lights on Main Street and the surrounding neighborhoods. Tía Serena even made her special Mexican hot chocolate, which Coral especially loved. Paired with some gingerbread, it was the perfect holiday dessert.

One evening after school had let out, Coral passed the guest room and heard her mother and Tía Serena talking behind the closed door. Being curious (and nosy), Coral pressed her ear to the door. A lot of what they said was muffled, but Coral could tell her aunt was crying. The longer Tía Serena stayed with them, the more likely it seemed her marriage might end. Coral's heart broke a little at the thought of it. She hated to see her aunt so sad and especially hated to hear her cry.

That night as Coral lay in bed, her thoughts swirled in a way she didn't like. She began to imagine what it would feel like if her own parents broke up too—how painful such a thing might be for her, Cami, and Matteo. As the sadness of the imagined thought almost brought tears to her eyes, she remembered to ask God for comfort and help.

Dear God, she prayed, *be with Tía Serena, and please be with my parents too.* As that prayer drifted through her thoughts, she also drifted off to sleep.

"Coral!" her mother called out the next morning. "Can you come to the kitchen for a minute?"

Coral did as her mother asked, taking another gingerbread cookie from a platter that was sitting on the kitchen counter.

"I need you to keep an eye on Cami while Serena and I run some errands," she said. "We won't be gone for long, and Matteo should be home in a couple of hours."

Being in charge of herself and Cami was a fairly new responsibility for Coral. "Do I . . . I mean, what should I do while you're gone?" she asked.

"Nothing in particular," Mom said. "Just keep an eye on your sister and call me if you need something."

Coral nodded and bit the head off her gingerbread man. "Okay, I guess," she said, feeling a little more nervous than she liked.

Mom shrugged on her coat and then squeezed Coral's shoulder. "You've got this, sweetie. I trust you, and you don't need to worry," she said, winking. Then she called out for Serena and reached for the car keys.

Once Coral's mom and aunt had pulled out of the driveway, she went and sat by her sister in the living room with the TV. Cami was so absorbed in a *Bluey* episode, she probably hadn't realized that the adults had left the premises. But as Coral plopped down onto the couch and finished off her cookie, her thoughts began to churn once more.

What if something happens and I don't know what to do?

Coral tried to focus on the TV show, but her mind went to a hundred different places—each one making her feel more and more alone. She bounced her legs up and down for a few minutes, then finally stood up and went back into the kitchen. Then she picked up the emergency cell phone off the counter and dialed her brother.

"Yup," Matteo answered in his trademark teenage boy way.

"Matteo, it's Coral. Can you come home already? Mom and Tía Serena left me to babysit Cami, but I . . . I'm just . . ." She paused, trying to collect her thoughts. Then everything came rushing out. "Do you think our parents are going to get divorced too?"

Matteo breathed a long sigh into the phone. "No, Coral, I don't," he said. "Are you really worried about that?"

Coral was trying hard not to cry and trying even harder to figure out why she was feeling this way. "I don't . . ." She paused, doing her best to name her feelings. "I'm just sad for Tía Serena and worried about bad things happening and just . . . I'm worried about being alone."

"Okay, okay," Matteo said in an uncharacteristically nice tone. "I'll get Oscar to drive me home. Be there in a few minutes."

Coral stood in the kitchen doorway counting the minutes until her brother made it home. When she heard the front door cracking open, she ran toward him, threw her arms around his waist, and buried her face in his puffer coat.

"Hey, kid!" he said, laughing and patting her head. "You didn't burn the place down yet, so I'd say you did a fine job being in charge."

For the next few minutes, Matteo was the best big brother ever. He told Coral that she was growing up, and that a big part of growing up was taking on new responsibilities. No, he assured her, their parents were not planning on splitting up. Finally, he reminded her that no matter what happened—good or bad—she still had a big family to take care of her and God on her side at all times.

"If you really think about it," Matteo said, "we're never alone, because God's with us. I can't really explain it well because God is kinda mysterious. But He is watching over us, and that makes me feel good. It should make you feel good too."

Coral nodded, and Matteo reached over to ruffle her dark hair. He laughed when he saw her hair sticking out in every direction, and she groaned in annoyance. Though her brother was irritating and moody sometimes, Coral was grateful for him—and for the God who had given him to her.

The next morning, the whole family, including Tía Serena, bundled up in their jackets and drove to church for the last service before Christmas. Coral skipped into her classroom and took a seat beside her friend Millie. On the other side of Millie sat a boy Coral recognized from school.

"Coral, have you met Luca?" Millie asked. "He goes to school with us and plays soccer with my brother."

Coral nodded and smiled. "Hi, Luca," she said. He reached out a hand to shake hers, the way a gentlemanly older man might.

"Nice to meet you, Coral," he said, pushing his shaggy, chocolate-colored hair away from his face.

Ms. Charlotte, their Sunday school teacher, called for everyone's attention and started the lesson by reading a passage from the book of Luke. Jesus, she said, had preached a sermon about God caring for every bird and flower. "God takes care of them. And you are worth much more than birds," she quoted. "Does anyone here like flowers or birds?"

Coral raised her hand high. Flowers, especially, were her favorite things to draw.

"The message here is that God cares for everything He has made," Ms. Charlotte said. "And when we are worried about something, we ought to remember that God is on our side and will take care of what we need."

Ms. Charlotte asked the class if anyone wanted to give an example of how God had taken care of them in the past. Though he hadn't said anything else in class, the new boy, Luca, raised his hand.

Ms. Charlotte pointed his way. "Yes, Luca?"

"Well, I was worried about my dad because he lost his job. He seemed really sad about it." Luca paused a moment before a big grin spread across his face. "But just this week he got another one. And he's really stoked about it too."

"That's wonderful news, Luca! Thanks for sharing. And it's a wonderful example because it reminds me"—Ms. Charlotte raised a finger into the air, her bangle bracelets jangling on her wrist—"sometimes we worry about our own lives and the lives of the people we love. But God wants you to give those worries to Him. Let's pray together and give all our worries to God as we put our faith in Him."

As Coral clasped her hands together and bowed her head, she listened to Ms. Charlotte's prayer. But in her heart, she added her own words too.

Father God, please take care of my tía. I don't know what plans you have for her and Tío Marco, but please help them. Help me to be a good niece to her, and help me to be a good daughter, friend, and sister too. Take care of my family, and thank You for being with me all the time. In Jesus' name, amen.

Later that night, as Coral's family sat around the dinner table, it began to snow. It was enough to make everyone rush outside to look. As Cami squealed and ran around the yard, Tía Serena came and wrapped an arm around Coral's shoulder.

"Tía Serena?" Coral said. "I prayed for you in church today."

Her aunt looked down at her and smiled, her eyes twinkling. "That means so much to me, Coral." She took a deep breath, and when she let it out, her breath turned frosty in the cold air. "I don't know what the future holds, but I know God is with me and taking care of me. And part of the way He takes care of me is through you. Thank you for your prayers, sweet girl. I love being your aunt."

Coral's heart warmed at her aunt's words. As Cami flopped into the snow to make a snow angel, and as Matteo laughed and nailed their dad in the shoulder with a snowball, Coral said another silent prayer, thanking God for all she had. She was starting to love her new home, and she felt a peace in her heart with her aunt by her side. God had been with her all along, just as He was with her now. He had made good things happen in her life—and He had so many more good things in store.

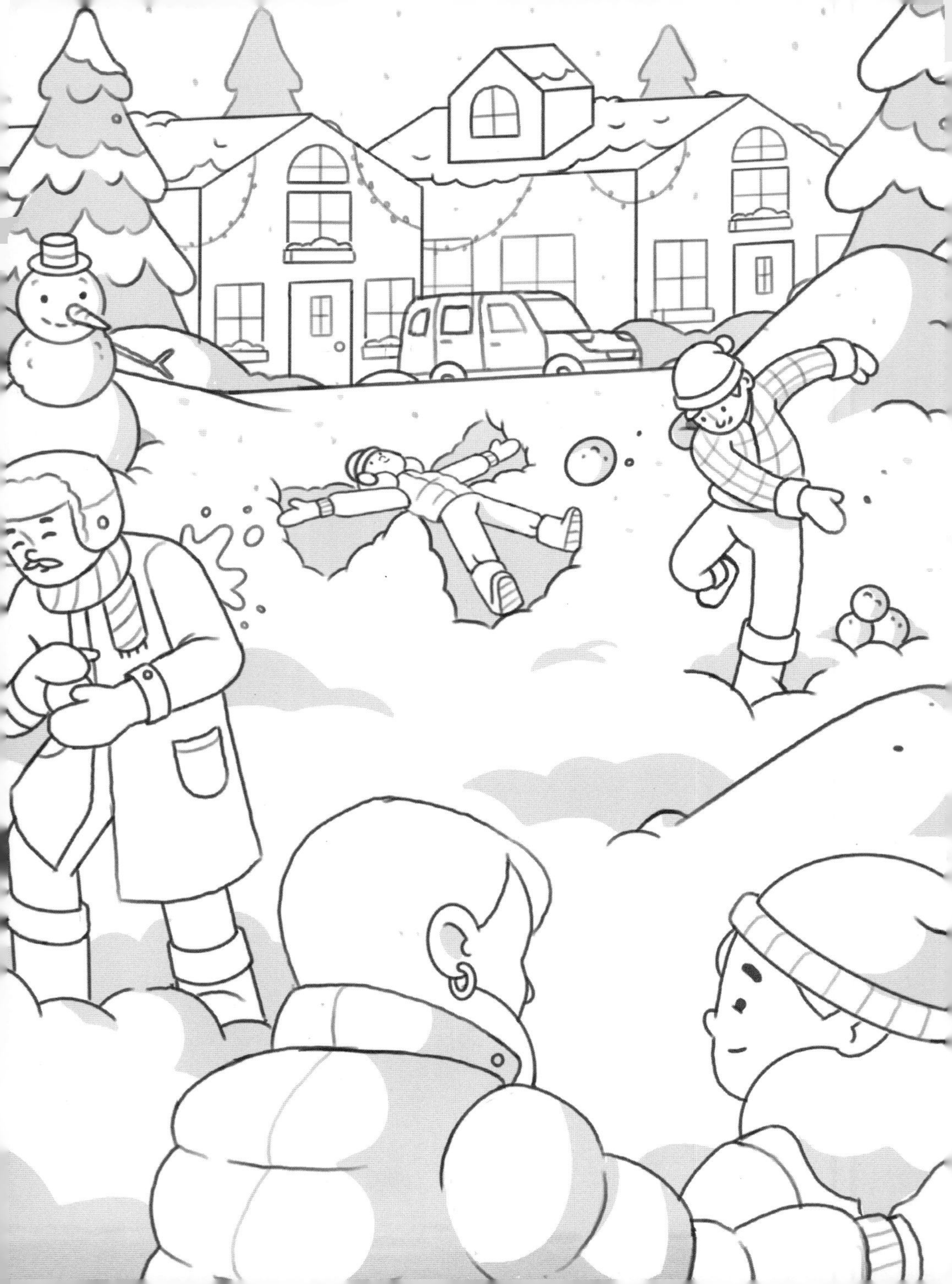

GET READY FOR BATTLE

As we've discussed, one of the most wonderful aspects of knowing God is learning how to trust Him with your worries and fears. But another way to build your trust in Him is to think about what He has *already* done for you—all the ways He's taken care of you and your loved ones in the past. Think of all the battles God has already helped you win. Naming these blessings will fill you with confidence in His strength, wisdom, and ability. And the next time you are filled with worries or doubts, young warrior, maybe you will more quickly be able to remember all the ways God has already cared for you.

Take a few moments now to name some things God has already done for you. What blessings are you grateful for? How is He providing for you today, and how has He shown His love to you in the past?

GOD HAS YOUR BACK

Young warrior, I want you to know how much I have enjoyed sharing all this with you. The book is over, but your mission has just begun. I can't fight this battle for you, but I'll be here anytime you need to pull this book out and go over it again. This is a journey you must be willing to take for yourself. I believe in you. You can do this. It won't be easy or fast or pain-free, but you can do this. I have faith in you, and God has got your back.

Can I say goodbye by saying one last prayer over you?

Dear God,

Thank You for the life of this brave young warrior. Fill this warrior with courage and strength to make good decisions and stand up for what is right. When their feelings seem too big or the obstacles before them seem too tall to overcome, remind them that with You on their side, they cannot lose.

May this young warrior always remember that You, God, are the One who moves mountains, heals the sick, and brings the dead back to life—and that Your love is so big and wide it can cover the whole universe.

Thank You for sending Jesus, Your Son.

In His name we pray, amen.

NOTES

Introduction

1. *True Grit*, directed by Henry Hathaway, featuring John Wayne, Glen Campbell, and Kim Darby (Paramount Pictures, 1969), film. John Wayne's character, Rooster Cogburn, said, "Courage is being scared to death but saddling up anyway."

Strategy 7: Choose to Be Brave

1. *MythBusters*, season 5, episode 3, "Underwater Car," directed by Alice Dallow and Tabitha Lentle, featuring Tory Belleci and Kari Byron, aired January 24, 2007, on Discovery Channel.
2. Jaemie Duminy, "How Many Times Can a Piece of Paper Be Folded?," Relatively Interesting, August 6, 2015, http://www.relativelyinteresting.com/how-many-times-can-you-really-fold-a-piece-of-paper-in-half/.
3. Joel Ryan, "How Tall Was Goliath and What Do We Really Know About Him?," Crosswalk, May 23, 2024, https://www.crosswalk.com/faith/bible-study/how-tall-was-goliath-what-do-we-really-know-about-goliath.html.
4. Chloe Merrell, "Basketball: The Tallest NBA Players in History—Full List," International Olympic Committee, November 4, 2024, https://olympics.com/en/news/basketball-tallest-nba-players-in-history-full-list.

Strategy 8: Plan for Life's Responsibilities

1. Mark Michaud, "Study Reveals Brain's Finely Tuned System of Energy Supply," University of Rochester Medical Center, August 7, 2016, accessed February 6, 2025, https://www.urmc.rochester.edu/news/story/study-reveals-brains-finely-tuned-system-of-energy-supply.
2. Amy Cuddy, "Your Body Language May Shape Who You Are," TED, YouTube, October 1, 2012, 21:03, https://www.youtube.com/watch?v=Ks-_Mh1QhMc.

Strategy 9: Give Your Worries to God

1. Britannica, "When Was the Bible Written?," last updated February 14, 2025, https://www.britannica.com/question/When-was-the-Bible-written.

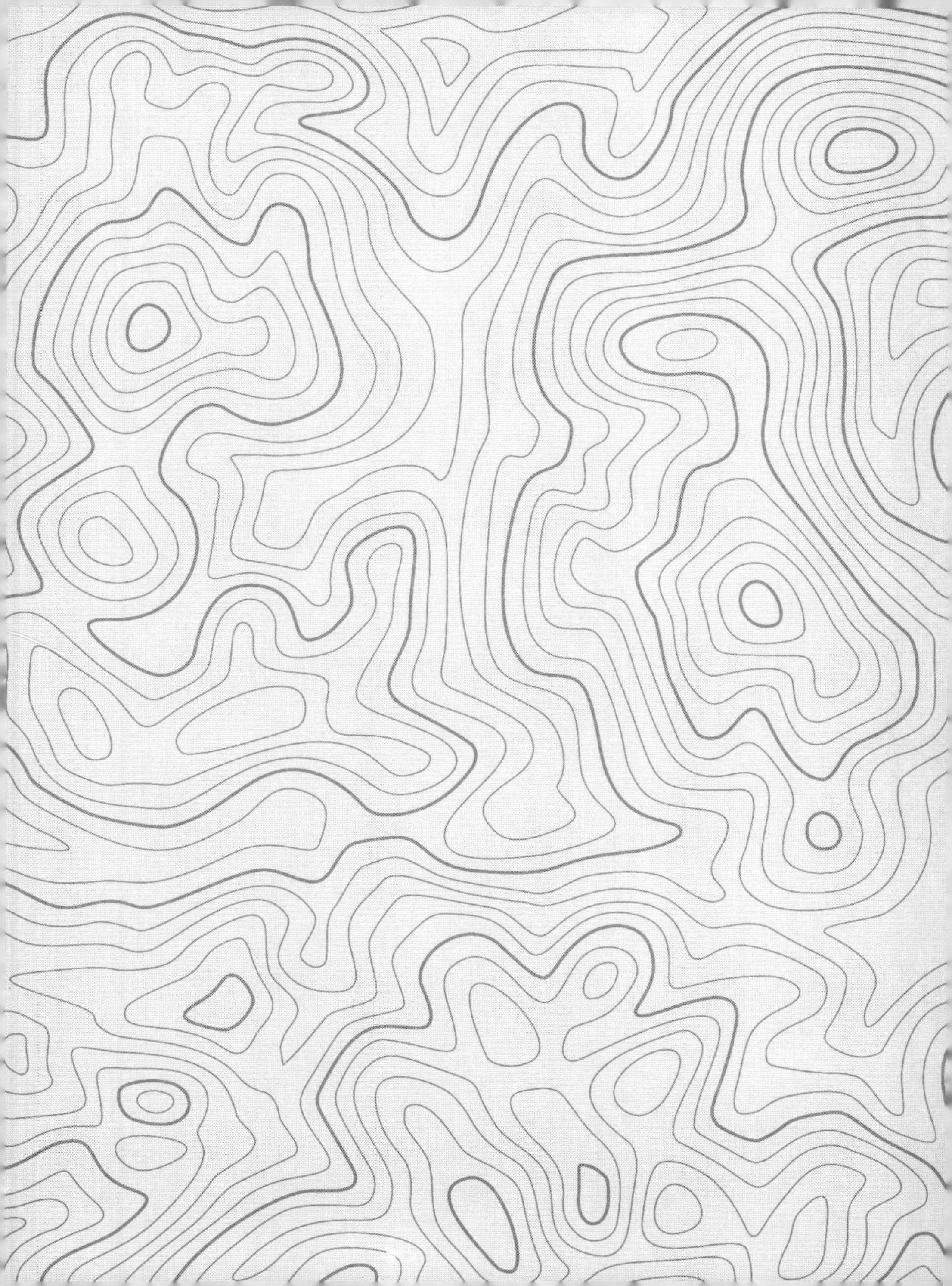